Who Are You?

Who Are You?

Michael Fuqua

Chapter 1: The Call

K eith looked down at his cell phone when he heard the second ring.

"Little brother," he said to himself. He wondered, *Does he need money? Is he in jail, or does he just want to tell me his latest trucker story?*

Several months earlier, his brother had called him, more than a little drunk, to share an observation he'd made about the mosquitos in Florida. "Keith, I swear to God, the mosquitos in Florida are so big they could fuck a full-grown turkey flat-footed. Yeah, boy. They're big 'uns," he'd said.

"Hey, Robbie Rob. How are you doing?" Keith said.

"You know I hate that damn nickname."

"Yes, I do. How are you, Robbie?"

"Fine. How ya doing, Keith?"

"I'm good. Driving down I-5 with the ocean on my right side and the moon shining high already. Beautiful night in Southern California."

"That sounds real good. Raining and cold here in Georgia. Been a wet winter. How was your winter?"

"Dry. Robbie, did you call me to get a weather report?"

There was a pause.

"Well, no. Uncle JB called me a couple of weeks ago. I hadn't heard one word from the bastard since I dropped Mama at his house. Hell, it must have been four or five years ago. You remember. Just after I brought her back to Georgia from New Jersey."

"That was six years ago, Robbie. What did he want?"

"Well, at first, he was bringing me up to speed on his health. His ticker ain't too good, and he's having trouble with his breathing. He's getting old, you know. Francis ain't doing much better. She's gotten pretty heavy, JB said. She's getting old too."

"I know. We are, too, and I've aged a year just listening to you. Now, what the fuck did he want?" Keith grumbled.

Robbie had a special knack for getting on his nerves.

"Well, I'm getting to it. Just don't get your panties in a wad."

Another pause.

"I'm listening, Robbie."

"JB told me that Mama's in a nursing home in Buchanan and that she's really sick."

"How sick?"

"Sick enough that he told me I need to go see her. He didn't come out and say, but he hinted that she might be dying and that she was asking for me."

"Well... did you?"

"Did I what?"

Exasperated, Keith raised his voice and said, "Did you go see her?"

"You ain't gotta yell. I ain't hard of hearing, you know."

"Okay. Sorry. Go on. Did you visit her?"

"Well, I wanted to know the whole story before I just opened my mouth and committed to going down there. I asked him what was wrong with her. Keith, she's got cancer. When he told me that she had cancer, I hightailed it down to Buchanan as soon as I could."

Robbie was always quick to respond to their mother's requests, but Keith found Robbie's responsiveness to their mother odd. The woman had put him in jail twice, and Robbie had walked into more than one brawl that resulted in getting beat up a couple of times. After July of 1975, Keith was slow to respond to any request from his mother. That time, he'd reluctantly helped rescue his mother after her apartment in New Jersey burned up in a fire—that she'd started.

"Yeah, go on."

"Well, I drove down there. Nice drive that day. No rain. When I got there, the people were real nice to Nancy and me. I took Nancy along for support. She handles things like this better than I do. A few months ago, her father got real sick, and she just jumped right in to help him. She's a fine woman. Best thing that's happened to me this year. We're getting along just fine. I don't like all her dogs, but she's a lot of fun, and she's damn good in bed if you know what I mean. You still have sex, or are you beyond that now?"

Keith took a deep breath, straightened up in his seat, and said slowly, "Robbie, what did you see when you saw Mama?"

"I'm getting to that. She was in bed and in pain. They're giving her big pills to control the pain. That's how bad it is. The nurse went up to her and said, 'Millie, you got a visitor. It's your son.' She opened her eyes wide, looked at me, and said, 'Well, Lord, Robbie. I'm glad you came.' I almost started crying. Keith, she's all shriveled up. Just an itty-bitty thing. She never was a big woman, but she has shrunk down to almost nothing."

"What's the prognosis?"

"The prog—what?"

"What type of cancer? What kind of cancer does she have?"

"I can't remember the name. They told me, but I don't remember. It's affecting her female parts if you know what I mean. At least that's where it started, but it's spread all over the place now."

Traffic was getting heavier as Keith was nearing his off-ramp.

Keith sighed, and a surge of sadness came over him. "How long does she have?"

"I asked them that same question."

Another pause.

"What was the reply, Robbie?"

Keith heard his brother take a deep breath. He sensed Robbie was choking up—on the verge of crying. Keith started to get a heavy feeling in his chest, and sadness was building. His brother drove him crazy, but Keith could feel his anguish.

"How long, Robbie?"

After collecting himself, Robbie said, "Weeks at the most. That's all. She's getting weaker, but all of her organs are still functioning. At least they are right now. Nancy said if you want to see her, you should get here soon."

"How far is Buchanan from Dallas?" Keith asked, already thinking about how to get there.

"It's about seventy-five miles. A little over an hour, depending on how hard you push it. There're a couple of little towns that are plumb famous for their speed traps between here and there. But I can show them to you on the map so you don't get caught up in one of them. You always did have a lead foot. That'll get you a ticket so fast it'll make your head swim down here. When you think you can get here? You can stay with me, you know. Nancy ain't moved in yet. We ain't talked about it, but it's crossed my mind. I just don't like her dogs. Right now, it's still just me in the house. Would love to have you. Been a while. You coming?"

Keith maneuvered through the red light at the bottom of the off-ramp and started on the last leg of his trip home from work.

"I got to look at my schedule and check on flights. If I do come, I'll take you up on your offer to stay with you. Have you been back to see her again?"

"No. We went down there last Monday. I call every day to check up on her. The lady who runs the place, Mrs. Nelson, is very nice. She thinks we have a little time. But I ain't been back. Don't think I will, either, unless you want me to come with you."

"What did she say to you?"

"Mrs. Nelson?"

"No, shithead. Mama. What did Mama say to you?"

"Not too much. She reached her hand out. I held it for a while. Introduced her to Nancy. Funny, she didn't seem the least bit interested in Nancy. Mama went on about how she needed her hair done and her fingernails polished. You know Mama."

"Yeah. Vain to the end."

"Yep, she is," Robbie said with a little chuckle.

"How did you end the visit?"

Robbie delayed his response a bit. Keith heard him take another deep breath, and Robbie replied, "Well, we just held hands for a little while. Finally, I said, 'Mama, we had best be heading home. I've got to work tomorrow.'"

"That was the last thing you said to her?"

"No. I told her that I loved her and gave her a hug. She put her arms around my neck and whispered, 'It was good to see you. Y'all come back soon. Hear?' I sat up with tears in my eyes, squeezed her hand, and left. Keith, it was hard. I think that will be the last time I'll ever see her." Choking sobs came through the phone, and Keith hesitated, unsure what to say. He could hear his little brother start to cry.

"It'll be okay, Robbie. Just hang in there. You did the right thing. I'm proud of you. Hey, I'm home now. As soon as I get my schedule together, I'll call you with the details. Give me a couple of days."

Composing himself, Robbie replied, "Okay. You be careful. Get here soon. I look forward to seeing you, big brother. I love you."

"I love you, too, Robbie. We'll talk soon."

Chapter 2: The Struggle Begins

Keith sat in his driveway for a few minutes, thinking over everything his brother had said. His mother was dying. He shook his head and got out of the car, heading in for the night. Walking through the front door, Keith was greeted by the usual welcoming party: a loud Pomeranian and three teacup toy poodles. Moving past the dogs, he put his briefcase into the hall closet and headed for the kitchen.

The dogs followed as though they were reminding him of his usual routine of reaching down, petting each one, and greeting them with their nicknames—Dipshit, Prissy, Sissy, and Candy-Ass. But that night, he ignored them.

As he finished preparing a double Tanqueray and tonic, he heard footsteps coming down the stairs.

His wife, Beth, entered the kitchen. "Hey, honey. How was work?" she asked. She looked at his glass and said, "Well, you going to pour me one too, or are you heading for the garage?"

"Oh, sure. You want wine or a cocktail?" Keith replied as he turned back toward the kitchen.

"Wine is fine. How was work today?"

"Oh yeah. Work was fine. Anything come in the mail?" Keith asked. He took a sip from his cocktail, put it on the counter, and moved toward the wine chiller. He reached into the cupboard, pulled out a tumbler, and started pouring the wine into it.

"Nothing much. Junk mail," she said. Then she looked at him curiously as she took the tumbler, half-full of wine. "This a new trend?"

"What?"

"Well, normally, wine is served in a wine glass, and cocktails are served in tumblers. It doesn't really matter, but it's different."

"Oh. Sorry. You want me to put it in a wine glass?"

"No. This is fine. You okay? You seem preoccupied."

Keith sat down on a barstool next to the island, took a big gulp of his drink, then put the glass on the granite top.

"Ah, something is wrong. You never put your glass on the countertop without a coaster," she said as she pulled one out of a drawer.

"Thanks," he said.

She took a sip of her wine, slurping a little at the end like she always did, as he continued staring into his glass. She put her glass down, said, "Well?" and continued to stare at him.

"'Well' what?"

"Are you going to tell me what's wrong?"

"I need another drink," he said as he got up to make another Tanqueray and tonic—a double—in a tumbler. As he was pouring, he said, "I got a call from Robbie as I was driving home."

"What did *he* want?" she said bitterly.

"Mama is sick. Robbie thinks this is the end."

"I'm sorry to hear that. What's wrong with her, and what does he want you to do about it?"

"That sounds mean-spirited, Beth," he said before taking a long drink of his cocktail.

"Sorry. But those rednecks have brought us nothing but trouble and grief. What's wrong with her?"

"Robbie says it's cancer."

"What kind?"

"He doesn't know, or he wasn't very specific. He said it started in her 'female parts' and has spread. It's all over her now, according to him."

Beth was no stranger to cancer. Four years earlier, her father found out he had liver cancer, then her mother was diagnosed with ovarian cancer. They died within two months of each other. It had been a tough time. Beth spent the entire summer in Coeur d'Alene, Idaho, watching both her parents die and fighting with her sister and brother-in-law over the will. That fight continued for nearly a year.

"That's a tough one. How is it he's only finding out about it now? If she's near the end, this has been going on for a while. How long has he known about it?"

"A little over a week. Uncle JB called him."

"Oh yeah, I remember him. I didn't realize stupid could come in such large packages until I met him. Pour me another glass of wine. I'm going to need it. This isn't going to be a good story."

Annoyed, Keith took the glass from her hand. For a second, he considered getting a wine glass for her, but he decided to just refill the tumbler.

"Here you go. You interested in hearing the rest?"

"I am now," she said as she took the glass from him. "Go ahead. So your uncle JB called your brother. Then what?" she said as she took a sip and looked at him with cold, piercing eyes.

"JB told Robbie she was dying and that if he wanted to see her before she died, he'd better do it soon. So, as he always has when Mama's been in trouble, Robbie jumped to it and went to see her the next day. Everything JB had told him was true. She's on heavy pain meds. She was conscious, kind of, and they talked for a short bit. He said his goodbyes and called me tonight. He told me that I should come soon. She doesn't have long."

A quiet came over the room as the two nursed their drinks and stared into their glasses. Neither looked at the other.

After another sip, Beth asked, "What are you going to do?"

"I'm going to go see her."

Beth moved away, walking farther into their kitchen and rummaging around the cupboards. With her back turned, she asked, "Why?"

"'Why' what?"

"Why would you want to go see her? What would you get out of it?"

"It's the right thing to do. She's my mother."

"The 'right thing' isn't something your family has a good grasp of. You've always been there for them, but all they've brought you is disappointment and pain. We have a lot going on around here. We need you."

"I would have thought you'd be more compassionate. It hasn't been that long. You were there for both of your parents. I was too. Of all people, I'd think you would understand."

"My relationship with my parents is nothing like the one you have with yours. You didn't have one with your mother, and rightfully so. Your relationship with your father is built mostly on your intense sense of obligation. No one would think of your relationship with him as balanced. You do all the giving. You give them all too much credit."

"He saved me."

"You saved yourself. You were nine years old. It was his obligation to take care of you. Morally, he had no choice. He did what he was supposed to do. Face it. He's a whoremonger, and your mother is a—"

"Stop! Just stop it. Think before you say anything more."

Keith expected her to get up and go to their bedroom to simmer. He felt a great urge to get up and go to the garage himself. But both just sat there. It wasn't clear what the next round would bring, but for the moment, they were in their respective corners thinking about the next move.

"Keith. You don't have an obligation to go see her. The usual rules and rituals don't apply here. You and your mother had no contact for twelve years. Then you saved her ass when she burned down her apartment in New Jersey. Your brother housed her, fed her, and put up with her shit for months. I know you gave him and her money to help. Lots of it too. You owe her nothing. We owe her nothing. Can't you see that?"

Keith's head was still in Pennsylvania, reliving the one night his mama had stayed at his house after the apartment fire. Robbie had driven her back to Georgia the next day. For a couple of months, she'd lived with Robbie and his roommate, "Snowman." Neither was easy to live with, and both drank too much. Mildred Louise Lanham-Clay-Smith-Harvey was smart, cunning, and manipulative when sober and a damn mean drunk. When Robbie couldn't take it anymore, he'd literally dropped her off in the driveway of her sister's house like he was dumping off a dog on the side of a country road. He hadn't heard a word from her since.

"We've been through this," Keith said absentmindedly.

"You're right, but you're still not getting it. You're blind with your weird sense of loyalty. Why in the fuck do you give a shit about two people who you've helped over and over again only to be disappointed? Please, try to see that I'm not trying to be mean. I'm simply saying that you don't have any obligation here. None."

Frustrated and a little confused, Keith got up and headed for the garage.

After the door between the utility room and garage closed, he turned on the radio, took a half-smoked cigar from the ashtray on the workbench, and lit it. After Keith took a puff and a sip of his gin and tonic, Beth came through the door.

"Keith, I'm sorry those words hurt, but they're true."

"Sure. I can't deny anything you described as far as the events go. Your mother, your father, your brother, and both your sisters are pros at cutting people out of their lives—particularly family. I've seen it time and time again over the last thirty-plus years. We were always careful about what we said to them for fear of them turning against us. It's a fucked-up fear, but fear is exactly what it was. We feared being cut off by your parents. I took shit from your father, and you took shit from both of them over the years, but we kept our mouths shut because we thought it might lead to them flipping the off switch on us. It was like the episode of *The Twilight Zone* where an entire village was afraid of the little boy who had the power to make people disappear if they said something upsetting around him. Now your parents are gone. None of your siblings joined us when we poured their ashes into the Pend Oreille River. Only their grandson and his wife bothered to join us. None of you have shared a word, an email—not even a text—since then. So I don't think you hold any moral high ground on judging me and my relationship with my parents."

"I'm not saying I have any ground. I know now that it could have and should have been different in my family. But my mother and father did a lot for us and for my brothers and sisters, too, so it isn't the same thing. Your parents have literally done nothing for you the entire time I've known you. They never did anything for our daughters—not even

11

birthday cards. And when I think about what you've done for your father and brother so many times, it just drives me crazy."

"Well, it ain't a long drive, and there ain't no risk of running out of gas, sweetheart," Keith said. He took a big puff of his cigar and followed with a long drink of his gin and tonic.

"Oh, you must be on your way to getting drunk or pissed. Your redneck is starting to come out."

"Both. The booze is delivering a good drunk, and you're pissing me off. There was a time you liked my redneck humor."

"Sometimes I still do. But right now, it ain't funny."

"*Isn't* funny. 'Ain't' is redneck. Remember?"

"Fuck you," she said, then turned to go back into the house.

Keith sat on the stool next to the workbench and took a deep breath.

***

The alarm sounded especially harsh when it went off at 5:45 a.m. Missing work was not an option. The cliché "You can't soar with the eagles if you hoot with the owls" popped into Keith's head.

"Yeah, that's just what you need. Start beating yourself up. That'll help. Coffee will help more," Keith mumbled. He got up, made coffee, showered, and got dressed. On his way to the office, he stopped at Starbucks for his fourth dose of caffeine. It wasn't even seven o'clock yet.

On the drive up the 5, he started to think about the conversation with his brother. When the call had ended, he'd known what he was going to do. Less than two hours after opening the front door of his house, he was no longer sure. At times during the argument with his wife, he was absolutely committed to going to Georgia to see his mother on her deathbed, if for no other reason than to spite his wife. But was that really smart? What did his heart tell him? What did he really want to do? As he took a sip from his tall Pike, he realized he didn't know. Time wasn't on his side. He had to figure it out either way and quickly.

His morning schedule was fairly light, but his afternoon was packed. After organizing the workday at his desk, he wandered down to Lynn's office. Lynn headed distribution and was the liaison between the plant in Monterrey, Mexico, and the distribution center in Dallas.

She was smart and dedicated. She also had a Keurig coffee maker in her office. He needed to talk with her and grab another cup of joe.

"Good morning. Can I steal a cup of coffee?"

"Sure. Go ahead," Lynn replied, looking up at him with her usual smile.

The two had been colleagues for nearly four years and had shared a lot of successes. After working and traveling together, they had gotten to know each other very well. She seemed to know his habits, thought processes, and moods. He knew a little about hers, but she was more mature and, therefore, was more of a mystery to him than he was to her. Keith found her fun to be with and attractive, but he was careful to keep those thoughts to himself—locked away. After picking up the cup full of coffee, he sat down in the chair in front of her desk.

"How are you today?" she asked.

"Good. We ready for the meeting with Monterrey this afternoon?"

"Yes. Here's the presentation. Finished it yesterday."

"Thanks." Keith took the slides and started going through them.

"Did you have happy hour with Bond last night?"

"What?"

"Did you and Bond go out after work yesterday? You look a little... tired."

"Yeah, let's call it tired. No, I got some bad news last night, and it led to a complicated evening."

"What bad news?"

Keith told her about the call from his brother and filled her in on the situation with his mother. He didn't go into the fight he'd had with his wife. The two had shared a lot with each other about their relationships with their spouses, but they didn't provide each other blow-by-blow playbacks of their arguments.

"Oh, Keith. I'm so sorry to hear that about your mother. Are you going back there?"

"Not sure. Still thinking about it. My mother and I, as you know, haven't exactly had a traditional relationship, so I'm conflicted about what to do. Robbie has always been closer to her, and I haven't seen her in years. So maybe him seeing her is all that's required. I don't even know what I would say to her."

"You have to go. She's your mother. It's the right thing to do. How can you even consider not going?"

"Well, on the surface, it sounds right to go. But when I really think about it, I feel like it's a shallow gesture. Just because 'it's the right thing to do' isn't enough."

"She's your mother, and you love her. You have to go. You'll never forgive yourself if you don't."

"I don't know that I love her. I love a woman who I remember as my mother, but honestly, the last time I saw her, I realized that I have almost no feelings for the person she is now."

"That's cold."

"Maybe. But it's the truth. I don't know why I'm telling you this. I apologize. I shouldn't have said so much."

"Stop that. We share things; it's what makes us such an effective team. We know a lot about each other. Sharing is good. But you must know that it would be a mistake not to visit your mother at what may be the end of her life. You'll regret it. I know you. I know you'll hurt later."

Keith's cell phone rang. "It's Bond. Got to take it. Thanks for the coffee."

Work pushed the conflicted thoughts and emotions about his mother to the side, at least for a while. A lot was going on. A new president had taken over. The new guy was a hard charger and was taking everyone's game up a notch or two. Keith liked the challenge, and he liked the fact that his team was up for the tasks, including several he had predicted and was ready for. Lynn was an essential part of the team and had played a big part in the group's successes.

As the day was winding down, he went to her office to review their meeting that afternoon. In reality, he wanted to continue their discussion.

"Hey. Nice job with the meeting," Keith said.

Lynn turned toward him and smiled. "Think so? The new guy makes me nervous, but he seemed happy with the numbers we showed him. Maybe he's just going easy on us."

"My read on him is that he's the real deal, and if he has a concern or question, he states it politely but directly. I know it's hard, but give yourself credit."

"Thanks. I'll work on that credit thing. You still deliberating about visiting your mother?"

"No. Haven't given it any more thought. What would visiting her achieve?"

"What do you mean 'achieve'? Visiting your dying mother isn't the same thing as solving a business problem. You get that, right? Oh yeah. I see now. It's a guy's way of thinking, huh?"

"It's an honest question. Whether I go or not, it won't change her condition, and it won't resolve any of the bad feelings or nasty history. I still think the truly honest thing to do is not go. Say a prayer for her, remember a positive moment, and carry on. Anything beyond that just seems contrived."

"Maybe. But it's the last opportunity for you to see her, and maybe it will bring her some level of joy."

"I can't say that any of the four or five times she and I were in the same room over the last thirty-seven years brought her any joy. They certainly didn't bring any to me."

"Did you fight?"

"No. Not really. Our discussions were uncomfortable, but we didn't fight in person. The best parts were superficial. We never dealt with the issues and bad blood between us. It seems that neither of us wanted to drag the past out into the light, and we both knew it was highly likely that a nasty fight would break out if we did. She has a quick wit, a short temper, and a sharp tongue."

"Oh, that sounds familiar."

"Funny. It's true, though. Our dark sides are eerily similar."

"You did tell me you fought with her a lot, but you only saw her a few times. When did you fight?"

"Over the phone. But those are stories for a different time." Looking at his watch, Keith stood up, then looked at Lynn and said, "I've got to go. See you tomorrow. Thanks for the chat."

"No problem. But I still think you ought to go to Georgia."

Keith smiled, turned, and walked out of the office.

About midway home, a call came in on his cell phone.

"Hey, Robbie. How are you? It's kind of late. You okay?"

"Yeah. Long day. When are you coming?"

"Don't know yet."

"What do you mean you 'don't know yet'?"

"I've got a lot on my plate right now, and I'm not sure what it would accomplish."

"You think too fucking much. What do you mean by that?"

"Just don't know what I want to do."

"Keith, just do the right thing."

"Yeah, that's one way to look at it. Why is that the right thing?"

"Wow. You're usually the one all high and mighty about shit like this. Listen to you. You're too smart for your own good. But you ain't got long to figure it out. No, you ain't got long. Figure it out, and do it fast. Call me when you decide something."

His brother hung up abruptly.

He thought about calling him back, but the urge quickly passed. Keith knew he had to make a choice soon.

Chapter 3: A Talk with an Old Friend

L ong commutes were normal for Keith. Since his junior year at CSUN and for most of his career, Keith had dealt with long commutes between home and school or between home and work. In California, Georgia, Wisconsin, Tennessee, Michigan, Washington, Pennsylvania, Illinois, and Ontario, Canada, it was all the same.

He had found ways to use that travel time early on. His usual approach was to think about work stuff for the first part of the drive home and about home issues during the last half. That process was reversed during the drive to work in the mornings. Pens and Post-it notes were readily available in the middle console to jot down thoughts and tasks when he came to stoplights or traffic came to a halt.

During a particularly rough stretch in his career and life, he had sought counseling to deal with his anger. His shrink had given him another idea to make good use of the commute. Following his psychiatrist's advice, Keith would imagine whoever was causing him angst to be in the windshield of the vehicle. Once the image was firmly fixed just below the rearview mirror, Keith would erupt into a long, loud, and nasty torrent of complaints and insults toward that person. It would go on for half an hour or so, depending on the source of his anger and the length of the commute.

But the usual approach wasn't working on his drive home that day. Keith was preoccupied with the question of whether he should go. His wife's nasty but honest words from the night before seemed to drown out the kind and thoughtful words from Lynn. A practice he found useful when he was dealing with a complicated problem was to get clear on what questions were relevant. One of his professors in graduate school had always said, "The journey to confirm you're working on the right problem begins by asking the right questions."

What are the right questions here? What am I trying to solve for? Keith wondered.

Pulling out the Post-its and a pen, he began to write down his questions: *Why go? What will it solve?*

What should I expect if I do go?

Is going only to avoid regret a good enough reason? If going won't hurt or help Mama, is there anyone else who might benefit or be hurt? Who? How? Why? If she's too far gone and won't even recognize me, then why go?

If she's not too far gone and is well enough to fight, and it all falls apart, then why go? What would it have accomplished?

In normal families, that moment would not just be about the person on their deathbed. Aunts, uncles, cousins, brothers, sisters, and parents would be active participants. That was not the case for Keith and his mother. Keith's parents had divorced thirty-seven years ago, and his mom went on to marry two men afterward.

The first man, Pete Smith, had owned a couple of used-car lots in Polk County, Georgia, and had a well-deserved reputation as a crooked man and a heavy drinker. Their relationship was almost as rough as the one she'd had with Keith's father, but it was shorter. Pete had died alone in a hotel room after a two-week bender brought on by the couple's last separation.

Edward Harvey, her third husband, painted houses for a living. They'd met in Georgia, but he was originally from New Jersey. After a couple of years in Georgia, the two moved to his home state. They fell off the grid. It hadn't bothered Keith and his brother, but their aunt Francis had grown concerned a year after the couple's departure and reached out to Keith to help find his mother. Reluctantly, Keith did.

He had started a search the old-fashioned way (it was pre-internet days) by calling the police departments in the towns he knew the couple had lived in. A sympathetic detective helped Keith find them, and Keith flew from Madison, Wisconsin, to New Jersey. He'd discovered them in a rundown government-subsidized apartment complex.

Edward didn't trust Keith's intentions and wouldn't allow Keith and his mother to speak alone, so Keith got the small skinny man drunk. When he passed out on the sofa, Keith had taken his mother to a local restaurant to talk. They barely spoke. It was odd. The only thing that came of it was that he had done what he'd promised his aunt: he told his mother that her sister was concerned about her. He'd only committed to finding his mother and telling her to call his aunt.

She drank a beer. He had a glass of wine. They ordered pizza to go. Once the pizza was ready, the two went back to the apartment and woke Edward up. Then Keith left. That was it.

Mildred Lanham-Clay-Smith-Harvey had lived in New Jersey with her third husband for more than a decade with very little communication with anyone—even her sister. Nearly twelve years later, after Edward died, Mildred lived alone in the projects. One night, she'd fallen asleep with a lit cigarette and caught the apartment on fire. She somehow managed to make contact with Keith's brother, and Keith helped Robbie get their mother out of New Jersey. After an evening at Keith's home in Pennsylvania, Robbie took her back to Georgia—home.

It didn't take long for the fighting to begin, so Robbie literally dropped her off at her sister's doorstep one Saturday morning. Since then, neither Keith nor Robbie had heard anything from her or about her for over six years. Then, the call happened.

Keith wrote down another question on a Post-it: *When did it go wrong?* After thinking about that question for a while, he wrote another one: *When was it ever right?*

Traffic slowed down, and Keith turned his attention to maneuvering through the jam. In front of him was a yellow '67 Cadillac. It reminded him of Fern's old Caddie.

"Yeah, that's who I need to call. Fern. She can help me get my head around this shit."

Fern and Keith had been friends since the days he'd worked for her delivering the *Herald Examiner* to liquor stores and paper machines all over Lancaster, California, when he was in college—over thirty-four years ago. So she knew the backstory of Keith's relationship with his mother.

Once he found Fern's number in his contacts, he called her. After four rings, he heard a loud voice come over the phone.

"Well, hello. How are you? When I looked down at my phone and I saw your number, I said to myself, 'This can't be Keith Clay. He never calls me. I always have to call him. But that's his number, so it must be him. He's either in trouble or feeling guilty, but he has a good excuse. Either way, it will be a good story 'cause Keith Clay tells good stories.' So get to it. Tell me a wonderful story, Keith."

"Hey, Fern. No excuses, but I do have a story that looks a lot like a problem that I want to share with you."

"Boy, you do talk purdy. Always have. Get to it. You have my full attention."

"Well, it's about my mother."

Keith gave her the details about the call from his brother and the conflict he was struggling with. As always, Fern listened intently, never interrupting Keith. When a pause presented itself, she jumped in and said, "Hold on, Keith. I think we need to talk about this in person. Come see me. Get your cute little ass on that motorcycle of yours Saturday morning and come over. Can you do that?"

After a moment, Keith replied, "Yeah, that's a great idea. I'll come up Saturday, the day after tomorrow. I can be there at nine a.m."

"Well, I ain't going to open the front door before ten thirty a.m. You can come up anytime you want, but you'll have to wait till I get up and make myself presentable. Normally, that moment doesn't come around until noon, but I'll commit to ten thirty for you, Keith."

"Okay. Ten thirty it is. See you then. Thank you, Fern."

"No need to thank me yet. Save it until I do something."

That Saturday morning, Keith got up and went through his usual routine. After coffee and feeding the cats and dogs, he went into the garage to get ready for the trip to Palmdale—about two and a half hours away. After putting on his cowboy boots and leather jacket, he poured himself a shot of tequila—his pre-ride ritual. Keith's wife came into the garage just as he finished the shot.

"You heading out already? Where are you headed?" she asked.

"I told you last night that I'm going to visit Fern today."

"Oh. Yeah. That was after my third margarita, but I do remember you mentioning it. Why? What's the occasion?"

"No occasion. Just want to see her and talk about this situation with my mother."

"Why? I thought we agreed that you don't need to go. It doesn't mean anything. Your brother is there, and no one will benefit from you going. Especially not you. It'll just bring you grief and inconvenience."

"I never agreed to anything."

"So you're going to Georgia?"

"I didn't say that. I haven't made up my mind yet. I want to talk to Fern about it, get her opinion."

"Doesn't my opinion mean anything?"

"Sure. I have yours. Now I want Fern's."

"So how many opinions are you going to get before you make up your mind?"

"As many as I need."

"Good. Get as many as you can. Take all the time you want. Eventually, you'll run out of time, and she'll be... well, you know what I mean. And you know I'm right. Nothing good will come of you going to see a woman you've seen just a few times in nearly forty years, and any contact you've had has just brought misery to both of us."

Keith turned back to the counter with the bottle of Don Julio and his shot glass sitting on top of it. He poured another shot and threw it down his throat fast while looking at his wife, then set the glass down and put the tequila in the cabinet. He looked over at her again and said, "Got to go. Be back around five."

He threw his leg over his black Harley Wide Glide, put on his helmet and sunglasses, and backed the bike out of the garage. At the bottom of the driveway, he started his motorcycle with a roar, put it in gear, and headed down the street, shifting hard and fast.

Once heading north on the 15, he moved into the fast lane and settled in for the long ride. Around him was the sound of wind rushing by his head. Below him, the pipes rumbled. Keith loved the roar of the engine almost as much as the sensation of speed. Since the prior summer, Keith had been making the ride to Fern's on the motorcycle. He drove his truck when the weather was foul.

Even though he and Fern had been friends for a very long time, they had lost track of each other for a a couple of years. One night on his way home, another dear friend, Sue, had called Keith and told him Fern had cancer. For a while, Keith made the drive from Carlsbad to Palmdale every other Saturday.

During the first visit, he and Fern had picked up where they left off. Talks with her were usually full of laughter, intense topics, and honest insights about themselves, each other, and life. There were very few pauses. Hours would pass by quickly.

Sometimes, they would go to lunch, but most of the time, they just sat in her small living room with Keith in a chair, Fern on the sofa, and Ed (an old boyfriend who'd moved in with her a few years prior) sitting in the corner by himself watching TV with the sound down low. It was odd how Fern talked about him and their roller-coaster relationship while he sat just a few feet away. But odd was the norm with Fern.

As Keith transitioned off the 15 and onto Highway 138, he thought about one of the questions he wrote on a Post-it: *When did it go wrong?* Shifting gears hard and fast as he started down 138, he thought, *Yeah, when did it go wrong?*

Was it when his mother cussed him out in the cheesy motel room in Lancaster on July 5, 1975? Just after Keith graduated high school, his parents split as planned. She went back to Georgia. She surprised everyone by showing up in California on the Fourth of July. Keith had just come back from seeing *Jaws* with a beautiful girl he had been pursuing.

Robbie came out of the house and ran over to Keith's VW Bug. "You drunk?" Robbie asked.

"No. Why?" Keith replied.

"Mama's at LAX, and Dad says we have to go get her."

"What? Where is he?"

"Jeannie's."

Keith got out of the car, went inside, and called his father at his new girlfriend's house.

Earlier that day, Keith had walked into the house after work to get ready for the date, and he'd heard his father on the phone cussing at someone. At one point, his father referred to the person on the phone as "Mildred." Keith went into his bedroom and picked up the receiver on the phone to listen in.

A woman on the other end sounded mad and drunk. Then, in the middle of a long rant, the woman suddenly stopped talking. Someone in the background asked, "Are you okay, ma'am?" Most likely, she'd passed out and fallen to the floor in the terminal.

Keith couldn't stop himself. He yelled, "Mama! You alright? Mama, answer me. Are you alright?"

After a few seconds, she was back on the phone and picked up where she left off with her rant.

Keith's father said, "Keith, get off the phone, son." So Keith hung up, showered, and left for his date. Then Keith knew what happened after he'd left his mother and father fighting over the phone. She had come back to California. His mother was back—already.

After several tries to reach his father at Jeannie's house, he finally got him on the phone. "You get that woman back on a plane to Georgia tomorrow. If you don't, I'll get on my motorcycle, and you'll never see my ass again," his father said almost instantly when he realized whom he was talking to.

Extreme behavior and events had long been the norm in their fucked-up little family, so Keith assumed his father was serious. Right then, he knew what he had to do. He hated it, but he knew. He grimaced, took a deep breath, and asked, "Where do I get the ticket? What should I do with her tonight?"

"I'll bring the ticket to the house. You put her in a hotel tonight and leave her there until it's time to go to the airport."

"Yes, sir." Keith hung up and walked back out to the VW Bug. Robbie was already in the passenger seat in front.

Keith and Robbie found their mother at LAX and took her to the Thunderbird Motel. She wanted to go home, but Keith told her the house was a mess and it would be better for her to stay at a motel.

She stayed there, but when no one was there the next morning to pick her up, she started calling the house every half hour, asking what was going on and demanding to be brought home. At first, Keith and Robbie made up a bunch of lame excuses, but eventually, they just stopped answering the phone.

As promised, his father brought the plane ticket to the house. Angry and confused about the whole situation, Keith asked him, "Why don't you take her to the airport, Dad?"

"I told you, son. I don't want to see her. You take care of this, or I'm out of here."

Not knowing what else to do, Keith took the ticket. "I want to take the bomb," he said, referring to his father's bright-red '67 Impala.

"Why?"

"I want to take Robbie, Martha, and Sherry with me. We won't all fit in the bug. Here're my keys to it. You take it, and I'll take the red bomb," Keith said. Keith had dated Sherry on and off for a few years, and Martha was Robbie's long-time girlfriend, so they both knew the boys' mother and agreed to help.

"Okay. Whatever you want." His father pulled out his wallet, took out three twenty-dollar bills, and handed them to Keith. "Here's some money for gas. It's low. Watch her get on the fucking airplane, and don't leave until it pulls away from the gate. Call me when you get back," his father said. Then the man threw the keys to the red bomb car on the kitchen table, turned, and left.

Keith and Robbie got in the car with Sherry and Martha, and they drove to the motel. When they arrived, Keith told everyone, "You stay here. I'll go in, explain everything, and bring her out."

All signaled agreement by saying nothing.

Keith walked up to his mother's room and knocked on the door.

A very angry drunk woman answered. "Where the fuck have you been?"

"How did you get the booze?"

"Liquor store, you fucking idiot. Where do you think I got it? To think you just finished high school. You're supposed to be the smart one."

Keith's mother had not attacked him like that in many years. Up until then, he'd felt sorry for her. After that, he didn't know what he felt. "Mama, I talked to Dad. He's bought you a plane ticket back to Georgia. The flight is at six. We have to go now."

She flipped out.

For the next few minutes, his mother cussed at him and told him he was worthless and stupid and was under his father's Rasputin-type spell. "You're just like your fucking worthless father. Only worse. You choose to be like him. He's just him. You *choose* to be like him, you little bastard."

It went on and on. Keith was hurt at first, but after a while, he just got mad—mad at his father for putting him in such a shitty situation and mad at his mother for being so mean. Keith had watched her drunken rants before and knew there wasn't anything he could do to stop it, so he chose to keep quiet and started gathering her things a little at a time while she walked around the small motel room screaming.

Keith assumed the girls and his brother heard the yelling and must've decided they wouldn't interrupt. When the yelling stopped for a moment, someone knocked on the door. Keith opened it, and when his mother saw the three standing at the door, she turned away from them and put her hands over her face. After a few moments of standing with her back to the group, she turned around, walked over to the bed, shut and fastened the latches on the suitcase, reached for her purse, and walked out of the door. Then, she climbed into the passenger seat without a word, leaving the suitcase outside the car.

Keith didn't know what to think of it at first.

Sherry broke the silence by saying to the group still in the room, "Let's go and get this over with."

No one said anything from the time they got in the car to the time their mother was on the plane. Only hand signals were used to indicate where they needed to go. At the check-in counter, the kids stayed back while the boys' mother checked in. Keith avoided making eye contact with his mother. Not even a "goodbye" was shared as she boarded the plane. As promised, Keith waited until the plane had pulled back from the gate. Keith let out a heavy sigh of relief, and his eyes watered as he watched it taxi away.

Keith's thoughts returned to the present. "Yeah, that was when it all went wrong for Keith and his mother," he said to himself as he shifted down to make the turn onto Fern's street.

Pulling onto the dirt driveway of the small stucco house in the desert, Keith raced the engine a couple of times to announce his arrival. After taking off his gear, he walked toward the front door and knocked.

Fern opened the door. She was standing there with the aid of her walker and said, "Well hello there, you handsome tall man. Come on in." Fern's smile was as inviting as her baby-blue eyes.

The eighty-two-year-old woman had been heavy the entire time Keith knew her. Pushing 240 pounds at five foot two, she embraced her weight as she did all her imperfections: with humor and honesty.

Keith had heard her ask before, "Do you want to see a short, fat old woman take off her clothes right here in front of you and everyone around us, or do you want to give me what I'm asking for?" The question usually had the desired effect. It was an effective negotiating tool.

Fern moved the walker out of the way, held out her arms, and said, "Give me a hug, boy. I love your hugs."

Keith bent down, put his arms around her shoulders and his right cheek against hers, and said, "Good to see you, Fern."

He followed her back into the house. Ed turned his head but didn't get up from his chair.

"Hello, Ed," Keith said as he moved to help Fern negotiate from the walker to her spot at the end of the sofa. Ed waved but said nothing. Keith settled into a chair directly in front of Fern. Fern asked about the ride, his daughters, and his wife.

Keith replied with a pleasant falsehood: "All fine. All good."

"Okay. Now, tell me about what's going on with your mother."

"You sure get right to it, don't you?" Keith said, smiling.

"Keith, I'm a fat eighty-two-year-old woman suffering from diabetes and fighting cancer. Ain't got much time to dawdle. So tell me what's going on."

Keith brought her up to speed on the call with his brother and the condition of his mother—or what he knew of her illness anyway.

"Well, what is it that's bothering you? Losing your mother? That's natural."

"No. I mean, yes. I'm bothered about losing my mother, sort of. But I lost her relationship-wise a long time ago."

"Yeah. You've told me the stories. But where's the doubt about going to see her coming from? Is it Beth?"

"She planted the seed of doubt. But it caused me to pause and really ask what the fuck I would accomplish."

"So the idea that it's just the right thing to do isn't enough?"

"To be honest, no. It isn't enough. Who says it's right? Why would going be right and not going be wrong?"

"Because I said it's right!"

Keith threw his arms in the air. "Fern, I love you, but you wouldn't accept that answer from me, and I think you'd be disappointed if I just accepted it from you and went."

"How's it wrong?"

"It isn't that it's wrong. It just isn't real. It isn't honest. We aren't going to resolve anything at this stage and in her condition."

Fern took a tissue from her bra, sighed, and asked, "Do you want to resolve things?"

"Sure, but I know that just isn't going to happen. Frankly, I don't even know what that would look like." Keith shrugged. "We had a rough life together, and our relationship was nasty at worse, estranged at best, after she and my dad broke up for the last time."

For over three hours, the two went back and forth. A couple of times, Ed tried to add his view, but he was cut off each time by a stone-cold glare from Fern. Talks with Fern, whether over the phone or in person, were always intense. Face-to-face was always the best, though.

She pressed from many different angles. She never lectured. She never scolded. She just asked questions with an agenda, a direction, and a plan. Keith always thought she would be a great chess player or lawyer. He envied her ability to ask questions and help him work through the issue he'd posed. Over the years, she'd helped Keith make some critical decisions. Like whether or not to remain married after learning of his wife's extramarital affairs. How that decision would work out was still to be seen. He and his wife didn't even share the same bed. She slept in the guest room and Keith in the master bedroom. It began as a way for Keith to get some sleep as her snoring became a problem, but the arrangement seemed to fit the stage their relationship was in. It became the new norm. It had been for over a year.

"Wow, Fern!" Keith said, looking at his watch. "I've got to be heading back. It's almost two thirty."

"Time does seem to kick into high gear when we visit, doesn't it?"

"It does. You stay in your seat. I can make my way out."

"Like hell, you will. I want to see that tall body of yours straddle that big black motorcycle and watch you shoot out of here like a bat out of hell. If I were forty years younger, I'd love to be on the back of that bike with you."

Keith walked over to help her as she stood up and moved her walker into position. She led the way to the front door, but Keith got to the door first and helped her maneuver the threshold.

Outside on the porch, Fern looked up at Keith and said, "I have one last question. How well do you know your mother?"

"What do you mean? She's my mother. I've known her all my life. I know everything about her."

"You do? Do you know everything about me?"

"No. I know a lot but not everything, I'm sure. What's your point?"

"Not sure. Just curious as to how well you really do know your mother. She's had her struggles, no doubt. She's made bad decisions or gone back into a lot of bad behaviors. I have too. You don't hold that against me, do you?"

Keith furrowed his brow. "No, of course not. You are who you are as a result of your decisions—good ones and bad ones."

"And you like me and have liked me for over thirty years."

"I love you, Fern. You're my best friend."

"When you heard I was sick, you came to me, didn't you?"

"Yes, of course."

"Why?"

"Because you're my friend. I love you."

Fern moved over to a chair on the porch and sat down, likely tired from the effort of walking to the door. "But I'm not blood. I'm a friend. I'm someone who loves you but not blood. But you came to me when I needed you. When I was in a dark place and alone, you came."

"Fern, that's different. We have a relationship. We've shared good times and bad times, tough decisions and challenges. We're more of a family than my blood family is. So it's not the same."

"Okay, you're right. But I'll leave you with one question: do you know your mother? You know what you experienced with her and what you think you missed out on, but what do you know about her?"

"She's my mother. I know enough about her to know that I can't help her. Never have helped her, really. I'll call you next week and will come back in a couple." Keith bent over and gave her a kiss on the cheek. Then, he walked over to the motorcycle, put his gear on, and sat on the bike. After he put on his sunglasses, he looked over at Fern, who stood on the front porch of the house, and started the engine. Both cylinders lit up with a bang. Keith put the bike in gear. Then he twisted the throttle a little and released the clutch slowly. Once he left the dirt driveway and was on the road, he opened the throttle wide open. For some reason, Fern liked that shit.

So did Keith.

Chapter 4: A Reason

When Keith stopped for gas on his way home, he checked his phone. A text from his wife read, *Jackie and I are going to the movies. Will you be home in time to go with us?*

Keith thought for a moment, then replied, *No. Just leaving. Go ahead.* Fern had filled his head with questions and thoughts—as usual. He wanted time to sort them all out.

A decision had to be made soon either way. If he was going, he'd have to make the arrangements and learn what he was walking into. And if he wasn't going, he'd have to explain to a few people—like his brother. Explaining to Lynn wouldn't be so simple, either, as she never let things like this go.

As expected, the Escalade was missing from the driveway when he pulled up. Keith quickly parked the bike, put his gear up, and turned the radio to his favorite classic rock station. Then, he lit a cigar and poured a generous double of Maker's Mark.

After taking a long swig of the bourbon and a deep draw of the cigar, Keith sat down to think about his decision. When the bike cooled down enough, Keith gathered a bottle of spray polish and a soft cloth and started cleaning the Harley. As he polished the bike, he thought about his talk with Fern. All the questions swirled in his head in a jumble of thoughts. A few days had passed since he got the news, and a lot of discussions had taken place, but he still wasn't sure what he was going to do.

In the time it took to wipe down the Harley, Keith went through all the options a million times with no conclusions. Eventually, his wife and daughter came home, and he finished cleaning up. Then he decided to sit in the hot tub and finish his cigar and another glass filled with two fingers of bourbon.

"Wow. Great idea," Beth said, coming onto the patio. "We'll join you." After a few minutes, she and his youngest daughter, Jackie, who was living with them after her divorce, got in the tub, too, both with a margarita in hand.

"So how is Fern?" his wife asked.

"Good. She looks strong. Now that she's off chemo, she's returning to normal, I think."

Beth swirled the water around with one hand, took a sip of her drink, and said, "Good thing she's always worn a wig so losing her hair wasn't a big deal, huh?"

"That's kind of insensitive, don't you think?"

"Maybe. Sorry." She shrugged. "But you know what I mean."

Keith sighed. "What movie did you two see?"

"*Hunger Games*."

"Yeah? What's that about?" Keith knew that question would be the topic of discussion for the next half hour. He was right.

Later, the group made tacos and settled in to watch TV together. After a while, Keith stood up and announced he was going to bed.

Keith climbed into bed after a shower, and images of his mother during different times in his life moved across his closed eyelids like scenes in a movie trailer: her taking a deep draw from a cigarette; her laughing and swinging on the porch at his grandparents' on a warm spring day; her sitting in the shallow water at the lake when she took Keith and his brother swimming; her posing for the camera during one of the frequent picture-taking sessions his father organized; and her riding bicycles with Keith, his brother, and his father.

"There were some good times," Keith said to himself as he rolled over on his side and slid into slumber.

At around 2:30 a.m., Keith got up for his routine trip to the bathroom, and when he climbed back into bed, Fern's question, "How well do you know your mother?" popped into his head.

"What *do* I know about the woman?" he asked himself.

He couldn't get the thought out of his mind, so he turned the lamp on, grabbed a pen and notepad, and started writing.

What I know about Mildred Louise Lanham:
Height—5'4"
Age—Not yet 73
Birthday—September 1939

"What day was she born?" he asked himself. He didn't know for sure.

Weight—He didn't know. She never talked about her age or weight.
Hobbies—Reading…

"Anything else?" He didn't know.

Favorite meal—He didn't know.
Favorite color—He didn't know.
Favorite movie—He didn't know.
Favorite song—He didn't know.
Favorite flower—He didn't know.
Favorite candy—He didn't know.

Keith kept writing questions and found himself writing "I don't know" or just putting a question mark instead of an answer. "I really don't know who she is," he said to himself after a while. The reality hit him that he had little time to get to know her if he really wanted to. "I guess that's it. I need to know who she is," he said to himself. "I *want* to know who she is. I really do. I want to know my mother." His eyes began to well up, and quietly, he began to cry tears of relief and pain all at the same time. Relief from the fact that he finally had a purpose, a reason to see her. Pain from the cruel fact that he knew so little about his mother, and she was dying.

For years, he hadn't thought of her as his mother. She was more like a wayward relative with vague connections to him and his life. He wanted to know who that woman, his mother, was.

After writing down a few more questions, he began to tire. So he stopped, put down the paper and pen, turned off the lamp, and went to sleep with a new direction that he felt good about.

He had a reason.

Chapter 5: "What's the situation?"

Sunday morning started cloudy and cool. Sitting at the kitchen island with coffee, Keith was enjoying the quiet time before the others came down.

After booking his flights to see his mother, he called Robbie.

"Hey, little brother," Keith said when Robbie answered.

"Hey, big brother. You're up early. I thought it was illegal to wake up before noon in California on the weekend."

"Funny. I'm still an early riser," Keith said. "Can you tell me again what home Mama's in?"

"Sure. Buchanan Nursing Home. Mrs. Nelson is the manager of the place. She's pretty nice."

"Mrs. Nelson. Okay. I'll call her tomorrow to get more information and set up a time to visit Mama."

"So you're coming! Good. When?"

"I get in Thursday. Got some meetings I can't get out of."

"That's okay," Robbie said. "You can stay with me. Just finished fixin' up the place. Would like you to see it. It'll be good to see you again and catch up."

"That works. I'm getting on an early flight into Atlanta, landing around four. I'll get the rental car and drive to your place," Keith said.

The two men continued to work out the details of Keith's arrival and getting to Robbie's house.

Once the logistics were out of the way, Robbie asked, "How long you planning to spend with Mama?"

Keith put his coffee cup on the counter, thinking about the question. "That's a funny question, Robbie. What do you mean?"

"Just curious. You have always been different than me on shit like this," Robbie said.

"Shit like what?"

"You go to funerals, you visited Maw Maw in the home before she died, and you told me how you talked with her a long time. Those things always depressed me. Hell, to be honest, they scare me. You come at this stuff different than me. I'm just curious about what you are thinking."

Keith took another sip of coffee and thought about his response. Then he said, "Couple of hours, I guess."

"A couple of hours? I was there fifteen minutes. What are you going to do for two hours?"

"I have questions. Nothing complicated. Just curious about her life. I'm not looking for some kind of reconciliation. Just want to visit with her a bit."

"That sounds good. But I've got to warn you, Mama may not be up to a long visit."

"Yeah, we'll see. I'll call you Wednesday to touch base. You be careful, and I'll see you Thursday night."

"Keith, I'm glad you decided to come. It's the right thing to do."

"I'm not coming because it's the right thing to do."

"Well, I don't give a shit why. I'm just glad you're coming."

"Thank you. Talk to you soon. Bye now."

"Bye, Keith."

***

On his way to work the next day, Keith called the assisted living home and connected with Mrs. Nelson. Southern accents come in a wide variety of styles, and hers suggested she was educated and was probably raised in a big city like Atlanta or Marietta. She said she remembered his little brother and had been expecting Keith's call.

Before he had time to ask questions, she went right into the details of how his mother came to the home and of her condition. Apparently, her sister, Francis, and brother-in-law, JB, had brought her to the home. Not long after she arrived, she was examined by a doctor, and they found out she had cancer. Mrs. Nelson suspected his mother, aunt, and uncle knew his mother had cancer before they brought her there.

"Why wouldn't they have said something before?" Keith asked.

"I don't know. Maybe they thought we wouldn't allow her to stay. But it doesn't matter. She's here now. The cancer is very advanced, and her time is short." She paused briefly, then asked, "When are you coming?"

"Friday. I'd like to be there first thing in the morning and spend as much time with her as I can. What are the visiting hours?"

"You can come in any time after eight a.m., and you can stay until eight p.m."

Keith thought for a moment, then asked, "How aware of her surroundings is she?"

"It comes and goes, but morning's when she's the most lucid. Your plan to come first thing works best."

"How is all this paid for?" he asked.

"I'm not at liberty to say," she said. "It's company policy to only share that information with those who have a legal obligation to know."

"So who has power of attorney over her?"

"Her sister and brother-in-law have legal authority. That much I can share but no more."

Keith huffed. "How often do they visit her?"

"They don't come during the week, so you'll have to call them and arrange for them to meet you here if you want to see them Friday."

"Do I have to notify them that I'm coming to visit her?"

"No, that isn't necessary for us. What you communicate to them is up to you. But we do require you to sign in at the front desk."

"Sure." Keith took a breath before asking, "What kind of cancer does she have?"

There was a pause like she was thinking about how or whether to answer. Finally, she said, "I think we should discuss that in person when you get here."

"Why the mystery?"

"No mystery. It would just be better if we discussed that when you're here. I hope you understand."

"I don't, but I respect your judgment. You've been very helpful. I'll see you Friday."

"I have you down in my appointment book for eight a.m. Friday."

"It might be closer to eight thirty. Can't judge traffic."

"If you're coming from Dallas, it's just country roads. Not much traffic in these parts."

"Okay. See you then."

After hanging up the phone, Keith wondered about the weird, mysterious response to the simple question of what type of cancer she had. Then, he began to think about the fact that his aunt and uncle had legal control over her life. He didn't trust them. The way they managed his grandfather's estate when he died and the nasty way they treated his grandmother after his death still spurred intense anger in Keith thirty-seven years later. Francis was the oldest daughter, and somehow, JB had convinced her father to name them as coexecutors of the will.

After his grandfather died, the sisters put their mother in a nursing home, only visiting her on holidays and her birthday, and Keith's mother took over the farmhouse his grandparents had shared for fifty-five years. They also sold four hundred acres of farmland along with all the farm equipment—plows, trailers, and the tractor that had killed his grandfather when it rolled over him, crushing his eighty-two-year-old body. Keith never knew where all the money went, but none of the grandchildren received a dime.

Money was the topic of the last discussion Keith had with his uncle, and it didn't go well. After Robbie moved their mother in with JB and Francis, JB called Keith looking for money. They were setting up his mother in a cheap apartment on the rough side of Cedartown, and his uncle called him to ask for money to buy furniture. Keith sensed that would just be the beginning of the requests. He put an abrupt end to the notion by reminding JB that he didn't have anything left after paying off the manager of the apartment complex to keep him from pressing charges against Keith's mother. Keith then went on to tell him, "I also know that once you tap my vein, you'll bleed me dry. That just ain't going to happen."

Both men cussed harshly at the other, and the call ended with Keith hanging up on his uncle. They hadn't spoken since.

Keith's mind moved to the summer visits at his aunt and uncle's house. Keith and his cousin Lanny had great fun riding their bicycles all around Cedartown, fishing and swimming on the river, and having root beer floats at the A&W near the house. But there was a dark side to the visits. His aunt Francis would take Keith to the side by himself and interrogate him about his parents and homelife. Then, she'd taunt and berate Keith about how his parents managed their money (or didn't manage it) and tell him how sad it was that he wasn't going to amount to much.

But the taunting and belittling weren't the worse things.

On the outside, JB, Francis, and their two sons, Lanny and Anthony, were the perfect Southern family. They had a beautiful big brick house atop a hill overlooking the little town they lived in. JB owned the local hardware store, they went to church every Sunday, and Francis worked at the boys' home. But Keith saw firsthand the brutality JB and Francis unleashed on Lanny and even on some of the orphans they brought to their house on occasion.

Keith remembered one brutal beating they gave Lanny when he accidentally dropped a glass of Kool-Aid on the patio just outside of the family room. Lanny was trying to open the sliding door to get into the house, and the glass slipped from his hand and burst into a dozen pieces when it hit the concrete. In an instant, his aunt came running through the door with a belt and began to beat Lanny with it. She didn't just lash Lanny with the leather portion of the belt on his bottom; she'd looped the leather end of the belt around her hand and started hitting him with the buckle on the head and neck as hard as she could over and over again. Lanny put his arms around his head to protect himself, but she was relentless and would find openings to aim the buckle toward. At one point, his ear began to bleed from one of the blows.

Keith thought she would stop when the blood started coming down his neck, but she kept beating Lanny. Lanny cried and screamed and tried to escape, but she cut off his path and kept hitting him ferociously until Keith and Anthony, both crying, begged her to stop.

When she stopped, Lanny collapsed in the fetal position, crying while blood oozed from his ear and from the back of his head.

Francis stood over him for a minute like an animal does over freshly killed prey. Then, she turned toward Keith and Anthony.

For a second, Keith thought she was going to start hitting him or Anthony. But she just looked at them for a second with the belt still in her hand and with her arms hanging straight down by her sides. The fight had gone out of her eyes. She looked tired, and she was out of breath. She moved the hair out of her eyes and said, "Anthony, go get a broom and dustpan and clean the glass up. Keith, help your cousin up and put him in the chair under the shade." Then, she went inside the house.

The same year Keith finished his MBA at Vanderbilt University, Lanny was sent to federal prison for drug dealing and money laundering. Keith got no pleasure from that fact and found himself feeling sorry for his cousin. It was a pity that Lanny had small-minded, pathetic parents.

Chapter 6: The Journey Back

Thursday morning, Keith dropped his briefcase off in his office and walked down the hall to Lynn's. "Good morning. Got the project all figured out?" Keith asked as he stepped over to the Keurig and made a cup of coffee.

"Not yet, but getting there. By virtue of the fact that you're here, I assume you've decided not to go to Georgia?"

Keith removed the cup of coffee and sat down in a chair in front of Lynn's desk.

"I'm flying back Thursday."

"Wow, that's wonderful! I'm seriously glad to hear that. What prompted the decision to go back?"

"Well, I went to visit my friend Fern in Palmdale on Saturday. As usual, she gave me a lot to think about."

"She told you that you should go back, didn't she?"

"Initially, yes. But I pushed back, and that prompted a long discussion. I won't bore you with the details, but it got me thinking."

"About what? How wrong it would be if you didn't go back? How this is probably the last time you'll have a chance to speak to your mother or see her—ever? How you'll regret it for the rest of your life if you don't go?" Lynn started counting on her fingers as she added,

"How bad a precedent you're setting to your daughters if you don't go? How—"

"Stop. I'm going. That's the important thing, right?"

"Yes, but now you have me curious. You were wrapped around the proverbial axle about how going back was just a weak, shallow, and meaningless gesture. Frankly, I'm really surprised you decided to go."

"Wow. You do listen, don't you?"

"Sometimes."

"Funny. Well, what I came to realize is that I don't know the woman. I started writing down questions about her that I had no answers to."

"What questions?"

"Basic ones. Favorite color, what foods she likes, what her favorite book is. Simple things like that. I just don't know her."

"So you're going back just to ask her what her favorite book is?"

Keith looked at her with a raised eyebrow, took a sip of coffee, and said, "Listen. My motivations and purpose are simple and real—at least to me. I'm going to visit a person I knew a long time ago who is now sick and very likely experiencing the last days of life. She happens to be my mother, but I know little about her. I want to know things. This is a chance to learn about her. I'm not interested in reconciling or forgiving. I just want to visit her and understand a little about her. That's my purpose."

"Excuse me, but that sounds a little selfish."

"Maybe. But it's more honest than going back to avoid regret or out of a feeling of obligation or fear of being criticized by others—like you or Fern. My head's clear, and my heart's satisfied with the desire to learn about her and maybe, just maybe, provide a lady with a little comfort."

"Why are you waiting until Thursday? How long will you be there?"

"We have a lot going on here, and I want to minimize my time away. I fly back Thursday and visit her on Friday. If need be, I can go back Saturday too. But I return to San Diego Sunday."

"Joe and I can handle the meetings. You should spend more time with your family."

"Thanks, but I'm good with what I have set up. I'll see you at the ten o'clock meeting." Keith got up and stepped toward the door. At the door, he stopped, turned to her, and said, "Lynn, I really do appreciate your input. You helped me think about this long and hard."

She looked up at him, smiled, and said, "You're most welcome. You're making the right decision."

Over the next few days, he jotted questions down he might ask his mother, some little, some big. He didn't judge them or think about them too hard. If a question came to him, he just wrote it down on a notepad he'd dedicated to that purpose.

Arriving home from work Wednesday night, Keith was pleasantly surprised to find both his daughters were home. They were in the kitchen with his wife, preparing a rare family dinner. His oldest daughter, Claire, lived with her boyfriend on a dilapidated horse ranch in the desert and didn't visit very often. Taking care of the animals and keeping the old buildings and equipment functional was more than a full-time job. Keith didn't really like how hard she had to work to have so little to show for it, but he accepted the fact that she had chosen that lifestyle and was even proud of her tenacity and focus. He just sometimes wished she'd applied it toward a different purpose.

"Hey, Claire. You come down from the hills to be part of civilization for a while?" Keith asked as he hugged her.

"Funny, Dad. Jackie told me you were heading back to Georgia to see your mother, and she and Mom wanted to have a family dinner before you left, so here I am."

"Wonderful," Keith said as he reached out to hug his youngest daughter. "Hey, sweetheart. How were classes today?"

"Good," Jackie said as she returned to the kitchen counter.

Keith said hello to his wife and gave her a peck on the cheek. He made a gin and tonic and started upstairs to pack. "Got to get organized for the trip. Yell when you guys are ready to eat."

He heard his wife say to the girls as he left, "I don't know why he's doing this. It's a waste of time and money."

Keith took a big swig of his drink and continued up the stairs.

***

When dinner was ready, the four sat down at the table. After a few minutes of small talk, Claire ventured into the topic that brought them all together: his trip to see his dying mother.

Claire asked, "How long will you be gone?"

"Fly out tomorrow morning and get back Sunday afternoon."

"When do you see Grandma?"

"Friday. I called the home Monday and made the arrangements."

"How is she?" Jackie chimed in.

"Not sure. I'll see for myself when I get there?"

"How is Uncle Robbie? Is he going with you?" Claire asked.

"He's okay. I'm staying with him, but he has to work, so I'll be visiting Mother on my own."

"How are things at the ranch and with Michael?" Beth asked Claire abruptly.

"Mom. We were talking about Dad's trip. I told you earlier that it's all good." Claire gave her mother a sour look and turned back to her father. "Does Grandpa know you're going to visit her?"

"Yes, I talked to him Tuesday. Can you pass the pepper?"

"Mom told me she has cancer," Claire said as she passed it. "What kind?"

"Don't know yet. The administrator I talked to wouldn't tell me. Robbie only told me that it was a female thing, but he didn't elaborate or didn't know. He's odd about stuff like that."

"He's odd about a hell a lot more than that," his wife said as she stabbed a piece of chicken, pushed it into her mouth, and followed it quickly with a big swig of wine.

Keith glared at her from across the table and said, "Enough of this. Jackie, tell us about your classes."

After a short pause, the message was received: the topic had been changed for the balance of the evening.

***

On the plane the next morning, Keith took out the notepad with the questions he intended to pose to his mother. After reading through them, he realized how random some were and how utterly stupid others seemed. For a minute, he started to think, *This whole thing is stupid.*

When the flight attendant brought him the mimosa he'd ordered, he took a long swig and looked out the window at the bright sun and the clouds below him. He started to visualize how the next day would go. He wanted to get a good, clear mental image of what would take place like he did when he was preparing for a negotiation or a presentation. He often found creating a clear visual of the moment helpful.

What does this look like? I know what I want from this. I want to know who she is and how she thinks about her life. But how do I do it? What if she doesn't want to talk to me? What if she doesn't even recognize me?

He paused. *Stop. Just stop. Breathe. Think it through. You'll deal with whatever comes. You know you can. You always do. You'll deal with it.*

When the second mimosa came, Keith began making notes about the visit and visualizing sitting beside his mother, quietly asking his open questions, then listening to her answers. He looked over the list of questions again.

***

"Hey, little brother!" Keith said when his brother opened the front door. He stepped inside, dropped his bags, and hugged Robbie.

Robbie stood at six feet one inch and was slim. Most truck drivers had pot bellies; Robbie didn't. A hat hid the fact that he was practically bald. He'd been a truck driver most of his adult life. For a brief time, he lost his license due to a crash, and until he got his license back, he worked construction and hated it.

Like their parents, Robbie had been married several times and had two boys from two of his wives. For the past twenty years, he'd been single but had many girlfriends. No relationship lasted more than a few months. The two brothers couldn't have been more different. Robbie was a bona fide redneck, blue-collar, Southern boy with simple and limited views on life, and he held little curiosity about what went on outside of the small town of Rockmart, Georgia. Like their father, Robbie was a loner. He had only one close friend, Snowman, that Keith knew of.

The old T-shirt Robbie was wearing exposed the long scar on his left arm, which had thirty-two pins holding the bone together. It was crushed when a truck Robbie had been working on rolled over his arm when he was nineteen. He also had a long scar on his belly where doctors removed his spleen after he got hit by a car when he was five years old. His right foot had numerous scars where a doctor sewed his foot back together when he was nine years old after he got it caught in the metal blade of a floor fan that was running on the highest setting without the protective screen.

Robbie wasn't reckless, just unlucky.

Under all the scars on his skin were even deeper ones. Robbie had seen and experienced more of his parents' violence and more of the long and loud arguments than Keith had. He'd also witnessed men "visiting" his mother when his father was at work, and the swapping that took place at parties had put deeper scars in his heart and soul. Keith saw some of it, too, but stayed away from the house as much as he could, working and doing anything that took him anywhere but home.

They never talked about how their dysfunctional family affected them. Keith just saw himself and Robbie as regular, hardworking people trying to move along. Strangely, he noticed they both had an ability to deal with chaos, conflict, and betrayal better than most. At least, that's what Keith told himself.

Robbie didn't like Keith's wife because he said, "She looks down that rich-bitch nose at me."

Robbie was right. She did. When they talked, Robbie always asked about Keith's daughters but never asked about or mentioned his wife. It wasn't uncomfortable or odd. It was just the way it was, and neither let it affect their relationship.

"Damn, it's good to see you," Robbie said. "Put your bags in the spare bedroom, and I'll pour us a drink." Any time Keith had business in Atlanta, he took time to visit his brother and one of their aunts.

Coming back into the kitchen, Keith said, "Place looks great. You've really done a nice job with the remodeling and decorating."

"Well, Nancy's the decorator. Her ideas, my money, sweat, and blood."

"Will I get to meet Nancy?"

"Yeah, I thought we'd go out to dinner Saturday. I asked her to come over around four. We'll introduce the two of you and go out. Snowman said he might come over too if he gets off the road in time."

"Sounds good. It's been a while since I've seen Snowman."

"So. You ready for tomorrow?"

"Yeah, I think so. I called the home and talked to Mrs. Nelson. I Googled the home and know where it is, and I read the reviews. They were pretty good. I've got my questions, and I know what I want to do. I think I'm ready."

"Questions for Mrs. Nelson?"

"No. Questions for M

"What questions do you have for Mama?"

"Just some stuff I wrote down."

"Let me see them."

"No, they're for Mama, not you."

"Come on. Let me see them. What kind of questions?"

Keith explained his plan and the nature of the questions and talked about how the idea came to him after his discussion with Fern.

Robbie sipped his bourbon and listened to his brother quietly and intently. "Wow, that's pretty neat," he said when Keith was done. "A little weird, but neat. How do you think she'll react to all that?"

"Don't know. We'll find out soon enough."

"Yep. Guess we will." Robbie gave Keith a look, then said, "Listen, I don't want you to be disappointed. Mama's in pretty rough shape. So don't expect much."

"Good to know. Say, what kind of cancer does she have? They told you, didn't they?"

"Yeah, but I didn't understand what they meant. I never paid much attention to what goes on inside of a woman. I know what I like and what's necessary, but I ain't no expert on a woman's parts."

Keith shrugged.

"Hey, I'm going to have one more drink, then I've got to crash," Robbie said. "You want another one?"

"Yeah, sure. Then I'll crash too."

Robbie made the drinks and came back into the living room. He gave his brother the glass of bourbon and said, "Here's to brothers. People come and people go, but we'll always have each other." The glasses clanged together, and they took a drink, then settled down to bring each other up to speed on jobs, cars, and sports—the usual.

After getting in bed, Keith took out his questions again and started thinking about how to start the process. *What if she isn't coherent or doesn't want to talk, or what if she gets angry and tells me to leave? What would be accomplished? All I would've done is anger a dying woman by intruding on her life during what are possibly her last days.* He flipped all the pages back to the beginning. *Fuck it. You're solving a problem you don't have yet. You'll deal with whatever comes.* He put down the pad, turned out the light, and went to sleep.

Chapter 7: "Who are you?"

The sound of Robbie's truck starting in the garage below woke Keith up at 5 a.m. In thirty minutes, his alarm would go off. Sleep had teased him throughout the night, but he was wide awake.

After making a pot of coffee and pouring a cup, he headed for the bathroom to shower and dress. When he got ready and stepped outside, it smelled like new flowers. The damp air was cool but not cold. Spring had officially arrived, according to the calendar. Outside, real signs of the new season were appearing, and to the east, a new sunrise was coming to life.

On the drive down to visit his mother, he thought about the last time he was in a nursing home. For several years, his paternal grandmother was in a nursing home in Chatsworth, and Keith would visit her when he was in Georgia on business. Grandma Clay had dementia and had lost her right leg due to an infection.

It was late afternoon on a weekday when he went to see her for what turned out to be the last time. Grandma Clay hadn't recognized him for a couple of years. Once, when he entered her room, she was awake, and when she saw him coming toward her bed, she started screaming, "No! No! Help me! Get out of here, D.! Go away! Go away! Leave me alone, you son of a bitch. Somebody help me!"

Keith froze in his tracks. A nurse pushed past him, moved to his grandmother's side, and started to reassure her and calm her down. "I think you should go," she said. "She thinks you're—"

Keith cut her off by saying, "I know who she thinks I am. I'm leaving now. Thank you."

D. was Keith's grandfather, William Daniel Clay. His grandparents had been divorced since 1959, just after she delivered her ninth child. D. left Keith's grandmother with seven kids still living at home. Grandma Clay raised the rest of her children by herself on the wages she earned as a laborer in a carpet mill. She lived a hard life. Dementia set in just after she retired, and the kids rightfully put her in a nursing home. She died not long after that last visit ten years ago.

Keith forced his mind back to the present, but for a moment, he wondered, *What if Mama looks at me and starts screaming?*

Keith made good time getting to Buchanan and followed the map to the single-story structure of Buchanan Nursing Home. The drive was pretty, with extensive farms and picturesque towns the whole way, lighting up slowly as the morning sun rose. When he walked up to the front entrance, he was greeted by an elderly Black man with a pleasant smile and bright eyes.

"Hello there, young man," the man said. "You here to visit somebody? You look like a doctor. You a doctor?"

"No, sir. Here to visit my mother," Keith said.

"Well, that's nice. You're a good boy, then. Go on inside and enjoy your visit," the man said as he pointed to the front door with his cane.

Keith smiled and entered the home.

A woman was just coming out of an office and walking toward the lobby when Keith entered. She was well-dressed and had shoulder-length brown hair with just a touch of gray. Looking over at Keith, she walked toward him with her hand extended. "I'll bet you're Keith Clay."

"Yes, I am. And you must be Mrs. Nelson," Keith replied, looking at her badge to confirm his assumption.

"Let's go to my office. Right this way," she said as she turned and started walking back.

"How is she?" Keith asked as he entered the small office and sat in a chair in front of her desk.

Mrs. Nelson sat down. Opening a file on her desk, she looked up and said, "Well, as your brother told you, she's very weak, she eats almost nothing, and the pain is getting worse. So she's not in a good place."

"I understand. What kind of cancer does she have?"

She looked at a note in the file. "Ovarian."

"How long ago was she diagnosed?"

"A few weeks ago, but it was very advanced when they found it."

"What about treatment?"

"Doctors said it had spread so far that treatment would be of no benefit."

Keith sighed. "How is she today?"

"Awake, and she had some juice this morning."

"How much time can I spend with her?"

"As long you want." Mrs. Nelson closed the file. "I can't guarantee she'll be able to stay awake long. When her pain comes, she'll want medication, and that often makes her sleep."

"I'll take what I can get. Can I see her now?"

"Of course. I'll take you down," she said as she rose from her chair.

Walking down the bright, wide hallway, Keith saw that the nursing home was very neat and clean. A few patients were in the hallway, either walking with a nurse or sitting in wheelchairs outside their rooms. Most of them were clean and had smiles on their faces, good signs they were well cared for. None were moaning or crying from pain. It was better than Keith expected, and he started smiling and saying hello to those who made eye contact with him.

Near the end of the hallway, they entered a room with three beds. His mother was in the bed closest to the window. Mrs. Nelson stepped to the end of the bed, looked down at the woman in it, and said, "Mrs. Harvey, your son Keith is here."

Keith stepped up beside Mrs. Nelson at the foot of his mother's bed, and the image of his mother came into focus. She was sitting up. The first thing he noticed was his mother's big blue eyes. They seemed too big for her face through her thick glasses. She looked up at him and smiled but said nothing.

Keith continued to stand at the end of the bed just looking at her. Her brown hair was freshly brushed and silhouetted her face. He smiled at her and breathed a sigh of relief at seeing her look so good. In fact, she was quite pretty. Far different from the last time he saw her.

His mother shifted her gaze from Mrs. Nelson to him. She looked at him with a quizzical expression on her face.

Keith thought, *She doesn't recognize me.*

"Mrs. Harvey, your son Keith came all the way from California to visit you," Mrs. Nelson said. "I'll bet you're glad to see him."

"Who?" his mother asked.

"Your son Keith. This is your oldest son," Mrs. Nelson explained.

To their surprise, Keith's mother said nothing but continued to stare at him. It was getting awkward.

"Do you know who this is, Mrs. Harvey?" Mrs. Nelson asked a little louder.

Keith's mother continued to look at him but said nothing.

"Is she on pain medication now?" Keith asked.

"We haven't given her any this morning. It must be the residual effects of what they gave her last night, I suppose," Mrs. Nelson said as she looked at the chart she'd picked up from the nurses' station. "I'm sorry you have to experience this."

"It's okay. All of this is better than I expected."

"But it's sad that she doesn't seem to recognize you."

"It's been nearly six years since I saw her last. Actually, we've only seen each other four times in nearly forty years. I barely recognize her." Keith twisted his hands. "Her eyes tell me she's my mother, but if I walked past her on the street, I might not know who she is. It's okay. At least she isn't screaming or afraid. Is it alright if I sit beside her?" he asked, pointing toward a chair near the bed.

"Absolutely," Mrs. Nelson said.

Keith moved slowly to the chair, positioned it closer to the bed, and sat down.

His mother continued to look at Mrs. Nelson, who was still standing at the foot of the bed.

Keith took out his notepad from his briefcase, and his mother looked over at him and smiled but still said nothing. He looked at Mrs. Nelson with a smile and said, "I think we're okay."

"It appears so. I'll let you two visit now. Press the button on the side of the bed if you need a nurse for anything. I'll check in with you later. Come see me before you leave, okay?" Mrs. Nelson asked while keeping an eye on Keith's mother. Then, she slowly turned and walked away.

Keith and his mother were alone. Sort of. The two other patients in the room lay quietly in their beds.

Keith didn't know how she would react if he called her "Mother," so he chose to call her by her first name. "How do you feel, Mildred?" Keith asked.

"Okay. How are you?" his mother asked.

Keith took that as a good sign. He pulled his chair a little closer. "Just fine. It's a pretty day outside, isn't it?" he asked, pointing toward the window and the ray of soft sunshine coming through.

"Yes, it is."

"Mildred, what's your middle name?"

"Louise. My middle name is Louise."

"That's pretty. Where did that name come from?"

"It was my grandmother's name. My mama's mama."

"Where did Mildred come from?"

"It was my daddy's mama's name."

"So your full name is Mildred Louise."

"Yes, I was born Mildred Louise Lanham."

Keith wrote her answer on his notepad. "Where were you born?" he continued.

"Aragon. Just down the road a piece."

Keith thought for a moment, then said, "There are no hospitals in Aragon. Weren't you born in Rockmart?"

"No, I was born at home. In our house." She shifted in her bed. "My grandmother and a midwife brought me into this world."

"Were you a healthy child?"

"Yes, I had to be to help around the house and the farm. But like Mama, I had spells sometimes."

Keith looked at her sharply and asked, "What kind of spells?"

"Sometimes my mama wouldn't want to come out of her room. She just lay in bed with the curtains drawn all day."

"You had days like that too? As a little girl?"

"Not until I was a teenager. But it wasn't fair."

"What do you mean?"

"Mama wouldn't let me lie in bed like she did."

"What would she do?" Keith asked as he moved closer to her.

"She would just make me get up and go on about my business."

"Did you ever talk about it with your mother or father?"

"No. That kind of talk wasn't allowed. We never talked about how we felt in our heads."

Keith wasn't sure where to go with this information. He wasn't a psychiatrist, but he was curious if this was when her emotional problems started.

"How long did the spells last when you had one?"

"Oh, I don't really remember," she said slowly.

"Do you still have them?"

"All my life."

"Did you ever see a doctor about the spells when you grew up?"

Up to that point, she had been sitting up in bed looking straight ahead at nothing in particular. In response to that question, she turned her head away and said, "Can we talk about something else?"

"Of course, Mildred. Who was the first boy you ever kissed?" he asked, hoping it wasn't too forward.

She turned her head around, and a big smile came to her face when she answered, "Bob Dan Gentry."

"How old were you?"

"Eleven. We were at one of my cousin's weddings playing hide-and-go-seek. Bob Dan found me hiding behind the fig tree by the smokehouse. I tried to run when he found me, but he caught me. And when he did, he turned me around and gave me a kiss on the lips."

"Did you enjoy it?"

She smiled. "Yes. Bob Dan was the cutest boy in all of Polk County, and he was two years older than me. I thought he was a doll."

Keith made a note on his pad, smiled, and asked, "Wasn't he a cousin too?"

"Yeah, but we were related to almost everybody in Aragon one way or another. It was a long time before I kissed another boy."

"Which one of your relatives was your least favorite?"

"Grandpa Lanham."

"You mean W. A. Lanham?"

"Yes."

"Why?"

"He was mean."

"Mean how?"

"He didn't like children much."

Keith furrowed his brow and looked up at her. "Didn't he have twelve?"

"Yes. But I reckon he was sick of children after having twelve and didn't want anything more to with them."

"Was he ever violent toward you?"

"No. He was just standoffish. I never hugged him or sat on his lap. When he visited, he made Mama, my sister Francis, and me stay in the kitchen or on the porch with Cathy May when it was pretty outside. I liked Cathy May. She would always bring candy when she visited. Grandfather brought nothing."

"Who was Cathy May?"

"His second wife."

Keith stopped for a moment. In a box of his grandfather's possessions, he had been given after his grandfather died, Keith found a prenuptial agreement between his great-grandfather and his second wife—Cathy May. It stated that she was to inherit nothing, and it was up to the children to determine how she would be cared for after he died. *Yes. I guess you could say he was standoffish*, Keith thought.

"Mildred, did your daddy whip you?" Keith asked.

"Lord, no. We would be sent to our room or given extra chores if we did something bad. Mama and Daddy never whipped us," she said slowly.

Keith looked at her and noticed her eyes were closed.

"Do you want to stop?"

"No. I like visiting."

"Who was your best friend as a kid?"

"Shirley Clay."

Keith was surprised to hear that name. Shirley was his father's oldest sister. He'd heard that Shirley introduced them, but he didn't know any more than that.

"How did you meet Shirley?" Keith asked.

"We sat next to each other in school. She was funny."

"Did she have any brothers or sisters?"

"Yes. There were eight Clay kids."

"Was she the oldest?"

"No. Bobby was the oldest."

Keith swallowed slowly. It had been a long time since he'd heard his father's name come out of his mother's mouth.

Before he asked the next question, Keith looked at her and noticed she had closed her eyes, her hands were gripping the rails on the side of the bed, and she was wincing as though she were in pain. He asked if she was okay, but his mother didn't respond. She just kept her eyes closed.

He hit the button to summon the nurse.

The nurse showed up almost instantly. Leaning over his mother, the nurse asked, "Are you in pain, Mrs. Harvey?"

Keith's mother nodded her head. The nurse turned to Keith and said she would be right back with pain medication.

Keith just stood there looking at his mother, admiring her freshly painted red fingernails.

It wasn't long at all before the nurse returned. From the wincing on his mother's face as the nurse tried to hand her the tablets, it was clear the pain was intense. When his mother raised her arms to try and take the tablets, Mildred screamed out from the shot of pain. The nurse gently put the tablets into his mother's mouth, placed a plastic cup with a straw close to her, and put the straw between her lips. His mother took a couple of sips, swallowed, and fell back into her bed, though she stayed in an upright position.

"Give her a minute, Mr. Clay," the nurse said. "She'll be okay, but we need to let her rest a minute or two and let the medication kick in."

"Will it knock her out?"

"No, I don't think so, but it will make her a little drowsy, and she may not be as coherent."

"I understand."

A deep sense of sadness and urgency hit Keith. He worried she was not going to be able to carry on that day. For a moment, he thought about leaving right then, but he thought better of it. And he didn't want to leave. In fact, he was enjoying the experience. His mother was in a clean place, she was getting good care from people who seemed kind, and she looked better than he ever expected. Yes, she was very thin and pale and only had a slight grip on what was going on around her, but it was still better than he expected.

Visiting with her was also giving him insight into her life. He was finally beginning to think of her as his mother and not just as the person who gave birth to him. His mother was lying in the bed in front of him. She was going to die soon. He knew that would be the last chance he'd have to learn anything about her from her own lips.

For a second, he felt like he would start crying, but he fought back the tears. *Man, get your shit together. You're all over the place. Settle down*, he thought.

Through the window, a bright ray of sunlight lit the room and gave it a warm, peaceful glow. Mildred dozed off.

Keith sat and watched her breathe; his eyes fixed on her red fingernails. His mind began to wander to the past.

"What'cha doing, Mama?" Keith asked. He'd entered the dining room and saw her sitting in a chair with a bottle of red fingernail polish, a bottle of polish remover, cotton balls, and a nail file on the table in front of her.

"Polishing my fingernails."

Keith picked up the bottle of polish and took a whiff. "Smells like my model-car glue."

"Put that down, son. You shouldn't be smelling this stuff. You aren't sniffing your model-car glue, are you?"

"No, Mama. Why would I do that?" Keith asked innocently.

"Just asking. Make sure you don't."

"Can I help you, Mama?"

"You mean you want to polish my nails for me?"

"I think so. It's kind of like painting, ain't it?"

"Isn't it. Yes, it's similar. Sit down, and I'll show you what to do."

Following his mother's instructions, the boy put the polish remover on a cotton ball, held her fingers, and wiped the old paint off carefully. As he worked, his mother asked him questions about school, his buddies, and even girls. "You got a girlfriend?" she asked.

"No, Mama."

"Is there a girl you're sweet on?"

Keith turned red and smiled.

"Well, now. I think I see the answer. What's her name?"

"Kathy. Kathy Scoggins. She lives up on the lake near Chuck Campbell."

"Well, that sounds nice. Do you and Kathy talk, or are you admiring her from afar?"

Keith rolled his eyes. "We talk, Mama. But I don't think she likes me because she barely talks back."

"Maybe she's just shy."

"Maybe."

"You know how to find out?"

Keith shrugged his shoulders.

"You ask her questions about herself, listen, then ask a little more. Then, tell her a little something about you."

"I can't do that, Mama."

"Sure you can. You can talk, can't you? What're you afraid of, son?"

"She might not like me back."

"Sweetheart, you're a fine young man with a big smile and an even bigger heart, and you're smart too. Worrying about what might happen isn't going to help. Girls expect the boy to take the initiative. So you take it, son. You take a deep breath, relax, and be yourself. You'll see. It'll be fine."

Coming back to the present, Keith remembered how that session had started a little routine between him and his mother. If Keith was in the house when she wanted to do her nails, his mother would ask him, "Want to give your mama one of your super-duper manicures, Keith? My nails are a mess and need your attention."

Keith had liked helping his mother and enjoyed their talks.

Keith saw his mother stir a bit. He asked, "You okay to keep talking?"

Without opening her eyes, the frail woman said, "Yes."

Keith could barely hear her. He stood and bent over to put his ear closer to her. "You sure you're okay to keep going?" Keith asked again.

"I like your voice," his mother said in a whisper.

Keith stood up for a minute, overcome with emotion. Turning away from the bed, he took three deep breaths and rubbed his eyes. After collecting himself again, he leaned over to her. With his face right next to his mother's, their foreheads almost touching and his eyes closed like hers, the visit continued in whispers.

"Did you know Bobby?"

"Yes, Shirley introduced him to me."

"Did he go to the same school?"

"Yes, for a short while."

"Were you and he friends?"

She was slow to respond. For a second, Keith opened his eyes and raised his head to make sure she was still breathing.

She was.

"Yes," she finally said.

"What do you remember about him?"

"He had a car. He taught me how to drive."

"Did your father know?"

"No." She laughed a little.

Keith could barely hear her, even with his head right next to hers. He took another deep breath and asked, "Was Bobby special to you?"

"Yes."

"What made him special?" Tears were starting to form in Keith's eyes again. He waited for the answer.

"Bobby was my boyfriend."

Keith's tears fell from his eyes to his mother's forehead. He sniffed and wiped the tear off her.

"Did you love him?"

After another pause that seemed to go forever, his mother replied faintly, "Yes. Still do."

Keith couldn't take it. He stood up quickly, dropped the notepad, and ran toward the restroom down the hall.

Inside the bathroom, he placed his elbows on the counter and began to cry out loud. Images of his mother and father kissing, holding hands, and laughing flashed through his head. The last picture of them together in the front yard of the house in California focused in his mind and stayed there. They were a handsome couple with great chemistry, and for a while, their passion for each other was intense and beautiful. Their relationship had ended a long time ago, but each still felt love for the other after all the years and all the disappointment, betrayal, and turmoil. Keith remembered his father often telling him that Keith's mother was his greatest love. And he was finally hearing for the first time, directly from his mother, that she loved his father—her Bobby.

It took several minutes for Keith to collect himself.

After one last wipe of the tears from his eyes, Keith returned to his mother's bedside. As he walked down the hall, a bad feeling came over him, and he started to run. In the room, his mother's eyes were closed, and her head was turned to the side.

Keith took a deep breath and grabbed his mother's hand. "Mama, are you okay?" Suddenly, he realized he'd called her Mama.

A few seconds passed.

No response.

"Mildred? Are you okay? Wake up, please." He felt her pulse and checked to see if she was breathing. She was, but he hit the nurse's button anyway.

The nurse came over quickly.

"I thought she had stopped breathing. Can you check her, please?" Keith asked.

The nurse checked her pulse, took off his mother's glasses, and looked into her eyes.

When the nurse opened his mother's eyes, she woke up and asked, "What's wrong?" in a low voice just above a whisper.

"Nothing, ma'am. You fell asleep, and we wanted to check on you," the nurse replied. Then, she turned to Keith and said, "Sir, the medication's kicked in, and she's probably not going to be good company for you."

"I understand. Maybe it's time to go. Can I just have another minute with her?" Keith asked.

"Yes, of course. Just come by the nurse's station to check out," she said. "Also, I think Mrs. Nelson wanted to see you before you leave."

Keith nodded and moved to stand by his mother again. Leaning over to speak into his mother's ear, he said, "Mildred, I have to leave now. I enjoyed our chat."

His mother looked up at him with her big blue eyes and smiled. She put her hand on his arm and said, "Okay. But you come back. I like visiting with you."

Fighting back the tears, Keith squeezed his mother's hand and looked at her. He scanned her face, her hair, her shoulders, and her hands, then looked back at her smile. He stood still and let the image of her sink deep into his mind and into his soul. It was his mother in that bed. She was beautiful.

Chapter 8: Taking It In

While walking down the hallway, Keith focused on the image of his mother. He didn't hear or respond to the nurses who said goodbye to him or the ones who said, "Y'all be sure to come back." He just walked steadily toward Mrs. Nelson's office.

When he stepped into her office, she stood up, walked around her desk, and held her hand out to shake his. "I know that was tough on you, but I think you brought a little relief to an ailing human being," she said. "Did she ever come to recognize who you were?"

"No, I don't think so. I suspect she thought I was a doctor." He smiled and looked down at his hands. "It really doesn't matter, though. We had a good talk."

"The nurses saw you stooped over her, whispering your questions. They said it was a beautiful sight." She paused. "How are you holding up?"

"I'm fine. Just fine. But I have to leave. I'll call you next week for an update."

She reached out and held his elbow. For a moment, Keith felt the urge to hug her, but he held off because he knew that he was on the verge of a massive cry, and hugging Mrs. Nelson just might trigger it.

Instead, he shook her hand, then turned and walked out of her office. As he stepped out onto the front porch, he looked around and noticed that the man who had greeted him was gone.

Looking up at the bright spring sun, Keith took a deep breath. It was a beautiful day.

He pulled his car onto the street and headed toward his brother's house. After a couple of turns, he was on the main road back to Dallas. Once on the highway, Keith began to replay the previous three hours back in his head.

A few minutes into the process, he began to cry. Initially, he thought he could handle it, but he was wrong. So he pulled over to the side of the road and stopped. Once stationary, he let it all out. Images of his mother—her hair, her fingernails, and those big blue eyes—were frozen in his mind. He learned so many things he'd never known about her.

But the thought that took the crying into full-out bawling was when she'd said she still loved his father.

For a while, Keith looked over the questions on his notepad and continued to cry. A few minutes passed, and Keith noticed traffic was picking up, so he wiped the tears from his eyes with his sleeves and looked at his watch. It was almost noon.

He felt drained, both physically and emotionally. "What do you do when you've just experienced the most beautiful moment in your whole life?" he asked himself out loud.

Then, to help him get his head on straight and pull himself from the confusing but beautiful state of mind, he asked, "Okay, if you had to explain this to a cold-blooded lawyer or accountant, what would you say?" It was a game he sometimes played when he needed to think about something in a different way. "You just spent three hours talking to a woman who didn't know you. You asked her simple questions about her life. None of the questions indicated that you knew her. They were questions you would ask an interesting person you'd just met at a dinner party." He sniffed. "You allowed an old lady to share pieces of her life with you, and maybe you made her feel a little better. At most, you got her mind off her condition and took her to pleasant places in her heart." Keith nodded. "So you're a good citizen. Get a grip, and get back on the road."

Keith put the notepad down, started the car, and guided it back onto the road.

A few miles went by, and he saw the big yellow arches of a McDonald's and pulled into the drive-through lane. He ate while he drove. A quarter pounder with cheese, some fries, and a Diet Coke were good for hangovers—both hangovers from drinking too much and emotional hangovers like the one he had right then.

Eventually, Keith approached the point where he could either turn slightly east and go back to his brother's house or continue north and go toward Cartersville, where there was a cigar bar he'd been to a couple of times when he visited his aunt Valinda. "Yeah, a bourbon, a cigar, and a phone call. That's what I need," he said.

Fortunately, it opened at 1 p.m., and it wouldn't be too busy that early in the day, even though it was Friday. Keith ordered a double Maker's Mark, bought a large-ring Maduro, and found a table next to a window where he could hold a conversation and enjoy his vices in peace. Taking out his cell phone, Keith texted Lynn: *Got time for a call?*

Yes! came the reply.

"Hi there," Lynn said in greeting. "How did it go?"

"Lynn, it was the most beautiful moment of my life."

"Well, tell me about it."

For the next hour, he did. Sitting next to the window with the cigar smoking in the ashtray and the glass of bourbon next to it, he started by explaining how beautiful the morning was, how clean and pleasant the home was, and how accommodating the staff was.

"All that is good," Lynn said. "Tell me about your mother. What did you ask her? What did she say?"

So he got to the meat of it. "Lynn, she was beautiful. Her hair was in sort of a bob, finely brushed and with no gray. It was odd. Her skin looked smoother than the last time I saw her. She must've quit smoking. Her fingernails were freshly painted and pretty. But she was very thin and frail." He shook his head. "Her, eyes though. Man, her eyes, Lynn. They were baby blue and bright. Given how thin she was and the glasses she wore, her eyes looked like they were too big for her head."

Keith pulled out his notes from his visit. "Her answers were fairly short but clear. Maybe she didn't have the strength to elaborate or didn't think it was necessary." He shrugged, then continued. "I don't know. At first, I could barely hear her, so I bent over the edge of the bed on my elbows and held my face next to hers so I could hear. Most of our time together was with our heads touching, my forehead against hers, or my ear close to her mouth." He paused and took a swig of bourbon. "It looked odd, I suppose, but it worked. Mama seemed comfortable with it."

"Did she recognize you?" Lynn asked.

"No. I think she thought I was a doctor with my sport coat and all. But it didn't matter. She showed no hesitation about answering. When she got tired, she would pause for a bit, but she never indicated she wanted to stop." Keith took a draw from the cigar and a big swig of his bourbon.

Then, he started to tell Lynn about his mother's answers about the family. When he got to the part about his aunt Shirley, tears pooled in his eyes, and he choked up. After a pause, he repeated what she'd said about his father.

There was another pause.

"Are you okay?" Lynn asked.

"Yeah. I just need a minute," Keith replied.

After describing how the visit ended, he welled up again and told her about pulling over and crying his eyes out. "Lynn, this was the best thing I've ever done in my life," he said. "It may sound strange. Some of it was painful, but the whole experience was more than I expected. Far more. Thank you for encouraging me to come and for being patient with my resistance. You're a good friend. I owe you."

"You owe me nothing," Lynn said. "What you did and how you did it is wonderful. You're a good son and a good human being. You did what you set out to do. You got to know her and gave her a little joy too." After a moment, she added, "Keith, I hate to do this, but I have a meeting with the warehouse lead and customer service on the promotion coming up. Sorry. Will you be back in the office Monday?"

"Yes, I fly back Sunday. I'll let you go. Thank you again," Keith said.

"Be careful and enjoy the rest of your time with your brother. See you Monday. Bye now." Lynn hung up.

The next swig of his bourbon emptied the glass. Looking up at the bartender, Keith signaled he wanted another. Images of Lynn sitting behind her desk and talking to him brought a smile to his face.

After finishing up at the cigar bar, Keith drove back to Robbie's house, but as he pulled up to the driveway, he saw Robbie wasn't home yet. Keith went into the kitchen, poured himself another bourbon, then went out onto the porch to call his father.

"So how did it go?" Keith's father asked.

"It was really good. She looked good, and—"

"What did she say about me? Did she ask about me?" his father asked sharply.

Maybe it was the bourbon, or maybe it was the fact that his discussion with his father was starting off so differently from the one he'd had with his mother that morning, but Keith had no patience for his father's ego. "Why do you care?" Keith asked, trying to sort out where his father was coming from.

"I just want to know what she said about me. Did she say anything nasty about me?"

"This isn't about you, Dad."

"I didn't say it was. I was just asking, son."

Keith threw his hands in the air. "All you give a shit about is what she thinks about you. You didn't even ask how she was or how she looked. The only fucking thing you think about is you. That's just plain shitty, old man. There are times when I wonder why I even bother with you. This is one of them."

"Hold on," his father said. "Get off your high horse, son. It was a simple question. Why are you being an asshole?"

"Because it comes naturally. I'm your fucking son, so I'm automatically an asshole. Like father, like son. Right, asshole?"

"You been drinking?"

"Having a drink when I talk to you helps me handle the ordeal."

"Wow. You really are an asshole. Maybe we should talk later."

"Yeah. Maybe." Keith hung up.

A minute later, he heard his brother's pickup pull into the driveway. Then, Robbie came onto the porch. The two brothers hugged and slapped each other's backs.

"How did it go?" Robbie asked.

"Let's order pizza, and I'll tell you while we eat."

"Good idea. I'll call the place up the street. They've got the best pizza on the planet," he said. "Grab me a beer, would you?"

"Sure."

Once they settled down with their drinks, Keith pulled out his notes and began to tell Robbie about his experience with their mother. He read the questions from his pad and repeated their mother's answers. When he got to the part about their father, he couldn't hold back the tears. For a few minutes, the two brothers hugged and cried together. Another beautiful moment.

For the rest of the evening, the two shared drinks, pizza, and cigars and took a grand trip down memory lane, which was somewhat prompted by songs from the classic rock station Robbie had on the radio. They explored every funny moment, every adventure, and a few not-so-pleasant events.

***

The next morning, Keith woke up to a loud ring coming from his work phone. Once he opened his eyes, he saw the sun was up, and his head throbbed with a hangover he knew would linger for the next twenty-four hours. Looking at the phone, he saw the call was from home.

"Oh shit," Keith said to himself as he hit the button to receive the call and put the phone to his ear. "Hello?"

"Have a good time with your redneck brother? Such a good time that you forgot to call home?" his wife asked on the other end of the phone.

"Sorry. Time got away from me."

"Yeah, right. You and your brother probably got shit-faced and were lost in your own little worlds."

"Something like that."

"Well, I'll be glad when this episode is over and you're out of Petticoat Junction."

"For the record, I'm in Dallas, Georgia."

Beth sighed. "How did your visit go with your mother? Is she really dying?"

"Fine, and yes. But she was coherent enough to have a good visit."

"Good." She paused, then said, "Why don't you come home today instead of tomorrow?"

"Because I want to spend some time with my brother."

"Why?"

"Listen, I'm in no condition to fight with you."

"Whose fault is that?"

"Mine." He cleared his throat, uncomfortable with the fact. "I'll call you when I get to the Atlanta airport in the morning. I have to get myself together."

"Good luck with that. Have fun," his wife said, and she hung up the phone.

Lying back down in the bed, Keith closed his eyes and took a deep breath. When he did, he smelled coffee. Slowly, he got up and made his way into the kitchen. Robbie stood on the back patio with a cup of coffee in one hand and a cigarette in another.

As Keith came through the sliding glass door and sat down with his own coffee, Robbie greeted him. "Good morning, Keith. How are you feeling?"

"Probably about as good as you, Robbie."

"Yeah, I hurt alright. Righteous drunk, though." Robbie laughed. "We should do that more often."

Keith groaned and took a sip.

For the next two hours, the two sat on the porch, having coffee and moaning from time to time. Finally, Robbie said, "Hey, I got an idea. Let's go over to Waffle House and get some hangover medication."

"Good idea. I'll shower, and we'll head out."

The weather had taken a turn, and it was raining and felt colder than the day before. Waffle House was busy, but the men found a seat. As they ate, they started to feel better. It was amazing how greasy food could cure a hangover.

As they finished breakfast, Keith said, "Hey, let's go visit Aunt Valinda." She was their dad's sister. Keith swallowed down the last piece of bacon and followed it up with a sip of coffee.

Robbie looked up at Keith and said, "No, I don't want to see anybody."

"Why?"

"Just don't. That's all."

"Okay. Then what *do* you want to do?"

"Anything but visiting relatives. I'm good with just hanging out at home with you. Nancy will be here around 4"

"Well, if you won't visit relatives who're alive, will you go with me to visit the dead ones?" Keith asked.

"What the fuck are you talking about?"

"Every time I come to Georgia, I visit all the grandparents' gravesites."

"That sounds like more fun than I deserve or can handle," Robbie scoffed. "Let's don't but say we did."

"Come on." Keith hit Robbie in the shoulder. "I'm going to whether you come or not. I'd like you to come with me."

"Well, let's do it the redneck way."

"What do you mean?"

"Let's get a six-pack first. Then I'll come with you."

"Deal. But I'll buy the beer. That brand you drink tastes like shit."

As they got up from the table, the two shook hands. Keith put twenty-five dollars under the bill, and they left the Waffle House. They stopped at a convenience store, and Keith bought a six-pack of Coors, a small bag of ice, and a foam cooler. "We'll toast each at the gravesites," he said as he put the beer in the back.

"The grandparents wouldn't approve of that shit," Robbie said.

"Grandpa Clay wouldn't want it any other way. We'll look the other way at the others' gravesites." Keith winked at his little brother and started the car.

For most of the morning, the sun periodically hid behind clouds. As they pulled up to the cemetery their grandfather Clay was buried in, the sun was in hiding.

"It figures it gets gray as we get closer to Grandpa's grave," Keith said as he pulled up. Standing by the marker with a beer in his hands, Keith looked up at his brother and said, "You liked the old man more than me. You want to say a few words?"

"What was your problem with him?"

"Other than being the meanest, most womanizing, biggest boozing redneck in all of northern Georgia, he had lots of appealing qualities. What did you see when you looked at him?"

Robbie looked down at the headstone, then at his brother, and raised his beer up toward Keith. "D. Clay was a hard man who lived a hard life. Some of that was by choice. Some was circumstance. But he made no excuses. He sought approval from no one. To Grandpa."

Each took a sip from their beers while looking at each other.

"You make him sound like a John Wayne character," Keith said.

"No, he wasn't a hero. He was good to me, and I enjoyed his company."

"He left his wife after she had their ninth child and there were still seven in the house. He did little to help Grandma or any of the kids." Keith paused. "He kicked me out of his house when I needed him most."

"You lied to him, and you were a runaway."

"I was fifteen, and I wanted to be in Georgia."

"You used him so you could be with Jeanette."

"Yeah, that's true. But he wasn't an adult trying to help a kid find his way. He was a selfish prick looking for a fight or a reason to show his perverted sense of power over me." Keith looked at his beer can like something on it would change how he felt. "But I didn't go home, and I didn't blame him for being him. I had bigger problems than Grandpa. He and Dad made me choose between being completely independent or dependent but in a warm bed." Keith sighed. "I thank both of them for teaching me hard lessons. But he was still a prick."

Robbie shrugged. "You and he got along pretty good before he died. Grandpa told me about your last visit. He bragged about you all the time. He thought you'd turned into a fine man, and he was proud that you got an education. Funny, he even bragged about how you called him from the airplane on your way back to Nashville. It blew his mind that you could do that, and it impressed him that you would bother."

Taking a swig from his beer, Keith took the words in. "I never held it against him," he said. "He was doing what he thought was best. I did hate him for it for a long time. But I figured if Dad could make an effort to get to know the man, I could too."

"To Grandpa Clay," Robbie said again as he raised his beer into the air.

Keith clanged his can against his brother's and said, "To Grandpa."

After the toast, Keith and Robbie drove a few miles west to Grandma Clay's grave. She was buried next to her mother and father.

In the same cemetery were two more generations of Smiths, which was her maiden name.

"It's fitting, isn't it?" Keith said as he drove.

"What is?"

"Grandpa's buried in a place where there are no relatives or even friends that I know of. Grandma's buried in a cemetery surrounded by relatives and friends from her childhood."

"He didn't care about that shit. He often said he'd rather be alone than with somebody he didn't care for," Robbie said.

"Yeah, Dad inherited that same attitude too. Dad still says the more he's around people, the more he likes dogs, and he doesn't really like dogs."

Keith paused for a moment, then asked suddenly, "Hey, have you talked with JB or Francis any more since you visited Mom?"

"No. Don't plan on it either. What are you thinking?"

Keith shrugged. "Nothing in particular. I was just wondering what kind of life Mama led living with or at least close to them." He glanced at Robbie before focusing on the road again. "Do you know if Mom lived alone or with them?"

"Don't know. Don't want to know. Don't really care either."

"That's pretty harsh."

"Oh, you have a good day with her, and now you're all gooey about her. She didn't even know who you were." Robbie huffed. "You were a kind voice in a dark place. That's all. Don't get all high and mighty on me."

"Hold on. Calm down," Keith said. "I'm just curious, that's all. I just thought you might've talked to them from time to time. You were always closer to Mom than I was."

"Three nasty fist fights with her husbands that she begged me to get her away from and then getting thrown in jail twice as a result of it cured me from the gooey 'love my mother no matter how big a bitch she is' disease pretty fucking quickly and permanently." Robbie pointed up ahead. "Hey, the turnoff for Crossroads Church is coming up. Slow down."

"They've really changed these roads around back here. I would've missed the turn. Thanks."

"Listen," Robbie said. "You had a good day with the woman. Keep that thought in your head and in your heart. But it doesn't change anything. Mama was a screwed-up woman."

"She's still alive. Can't talk about her in the past tense yet." Keith raised his eyebrows a bit. "Besides, I got my head around it all. I'm just curious about how she got the way she did. Aren't you?"

"Fuck no." Robbie nodded toward another road. "Up ahead on the right."

"Got it."

Keith knew where their grandmother's gravesite was, so they headed straight there, and just as they pulled up next to it, the skies opened up, and it started to pour rain.

"Well, let's toast to Grandma Clay here in the car, and maybe the rain will let up and we can get out to say hello to her in a bit," Keith said as he put the car in park.

Reaching behind Keith's seat, Robbie grabbed two more beers from the cooler. "You been living in California too long. You're starting to sound weird," Robbie said as he handed Keith a beer.

"To Grandma Clay," Keith said. "Life dealt her more than her share of struggles, but she worked hard, raised most of her kids on her own, and stayed true to herself and to her faith. God, you got the best humankind has to offer." He looked at his brother, and they clanged the cans together and took big swigs.

The clouds weren't moving, and they seemed to have an endless reservoir of water. The rain was still coming down when they'd finished their drinks, so they decided to continue to the cemetery their mother's parents were buried in.

Oak Ridge Baptist Church was a small white church a few miles outside of Aragon. It sat at the base of a mountain with a stream running nearby. Keith always thought it was a beautiful place, and he was grateful his favorite grandparents were placed there for eternity.

All the clouds that brought the rain were heading east, and Oak Ridge Baptist Church was west, so they left the rain behind them. Clouds still hid the sun, but it wasn't raining anymore.

Walking along the pathway to the gravesites, Robbie looked around at the names on the headstones and said, "A lot of Gentrys and Smiths in this cemetery. Grandma and Grandpa are the only Lanhams. Wonder why."

"Really? There are more Smiths and Gentrys in these parts than Lanhams?" Keith replied.

Robbie flipped his brother off.

"Hey, it's okay. I'm just glad you're curious about something. See, ain't curiosity a good thing?"

Robbie looked at Keith with a furrowed brow and flipped him off again.

"Wow, she was only sixteen when they got married," Robbie said as he stared at the headstones of Phillip and Ethyl Lanham. "He was twenty-five."

"Grandma was thirty-eight before she had Aunt Francis," Keith added. "During my last visit with her, I asked her why they waited so long to have children. She said that it wasn't her intention and that 'God just set it up that way.' I've often wondered if having children that late in life might be part of the reason both the girls were a little on the emotionally frail side."

"That's a kind way of saying the two girls are batshit crazy," Robbie said.

Keith shrugged. "Even if the girls were crazy, Grandpa was someone I truly respected and looked up to. He was a World War One veteran, a successful farmer, and a leader in this little church. I remember coming to church with him during my summer visits. He sat in the pews behind the preacher with the other elders." Keith chuckled. "Not once did I see him fall asleep like a lot of the old men did. I was always proud of my Paw Paw," he said as he looked down at the headstone.

"Me too. But I didn't spend as much time with them as you did."

"Do you remember when we lived with them for a while when Mom and Dad split up the first time? It was tough."

"Not much. I was only five."

"It was a tough time."

Robbie looked at his watch. "Can we go soon?" he asked, changing the subject. "I think I've had enough of graveyards," Robbie said.

Keith looked at him and noticed that Robbie's eyes were watering. Looking down at his watch, Keith said, "Yeah. It's time we head back if we're going to meet Snowman for dinner. But we've got to toast Paw Paw and Maw Maw before we leave." They raised their drinks, then got in the car to go meet up with Robbie's friend.

Silence lingered through most of the drive back until Robbie said, "I wonder where they are going to bury Mama."

"Well, she isn't dead yet," Keith replied.

"Keith, she's dying as we speak. You know that, right?"

Keith sighed. "Yeah. I know that."

"So what are you thinking?"

"Nothing. We don't know how close she is. That's all. Maybe we have more time."

"More time for what?" Robbie asked.

"I don't know. Just maybe we have more time."

"Keith, I don't know what you're thinking or why, but you need to get your head around the fact that the next time you visit Mama, it'll be in a cemetery. Cold, I know. And it's hard. But it's the truth."

Keith heard the words, decided not to argue, and just let it go.

***

Sunday morning came, but luckily, without the hangover he'd woken up with the morning before. Robbie got up early, too, and made eggs and sausage for breakfast. During breakfast, they talked about the workweek ahead for both of them, unsure of how to say goodbye. After putting the dishes in the dishwasher, Keith gathered his things.

As the two walked outside toward Keith's rental car, Robbie said, "Going to miss you, big brother. It's great to see you again. When do you think you'll be back this way?"

"Don't know. Soon maybe." Keith shrugged. "I'll see what I can work out and let you know."

"Good. I'll call you if anything happens with Mama."

"Okay. Thanks, Robbie. I love you."

"Love you too, Keith. Drive safe and text me when you get home."

Keith got in the car and made his way to the airport. Along his drive, he noticed how clear the skies were and how bright and warm the sun felt. It reminded him of his morning trip to Buchanan. It was a beautiful day and a beautiful moment.

He allowed himself to replay the steps, words, and emotions of his time with his mother. And those thoughts continued as he went through security and into the terminal. Once inside, he went to the Admiral's Club, got settled, and called home.

"Good morning," his wife said when she answered. "You at the airport?"

"Yes."

"Good visit?"

"Yeah. Robbie and I visited our grandparents' gravesites and had dinner with his girlfriend and his old friend Snowman last night."

"Oh." She laughed. "I still don't understand why everyone goes by their nicknames down there."

"It was his handle when he drove trucks with Robbie," Keith said, fiddling with his shirt.

"That clears it up nicely. What time do you land?"

"Around four. Home by five."

"Good. I'm glad this is coming to an end."

Keith furrowed his eyebrows. "What do you mean?"

"Well, you know." His wife took a breath. "You wanted to see your mother for the last time. You did. You wanted to spend time with your brother. You did. Now you can come home where you belong."

"Okay." Keith sighed, then continued. "Listen, I've got to take care of a couple of emails before I get on the plane. See you when I get home."

"Okay. Bye."

Keith put the phone away and reached for his briefcase next to his chair. But instead of grabbing his laptop, he pulled out the notepad with the questions he'd asked his mother. As he read through them, he made notes of her replies.

Then, he thought, *How did she become the troubled woman I knew most of my life?*

He began writing more questions.

Chapter 9: A Return?

Keith met up with his boss, Mike, first thing the next day. He gave Mike a synopsis of his visit with his mother and shared his plans for a second trip the following week.

"Keith, are you forgetting the trip to China and then to Brisbane? We've been planning this trip to Zhongshan for weeks, and the Australia problem is getting bigger," Mike said. "I've got to be honest. It will be a big problem if you don't go."

Mike and Keith were not only work colleagues but were also good friends. For nearly fifteen years, the two had gotten to know each other, enjoyed success together, and helped each other through difficult times. Both were good at turnarounds and managing large, complicated projects. Outside of work, they and their wives spent a lot of time together. Each knew how the other thought, and they trusted each other implicitly.

Keith didn't seek counsel from many, but Mike was at the top of the list of people whose opinions he valued. In his heart, he knew Mike's assessments were correct. But his heart was having a hard time processing the message.

"Okay," Keith finally said. "Then I'll take the rest of this week off and get back Saturday. We don't leave until Sunday."

"Man, I get what you're going through, but as a friend, not your boss, think about what you're doing. We've got the decision on the new system facing us this week, and Todd would be concerned if you weren't part of that." Mike paused. "Keith, I know you, and I know the history with your family, particularly with your mother. It's wonderful that you had a good moment with her. Maybe it's best to let that one be the memory you carry with you." He took a deep breath and said, "Man, she isn't getting better. Time's not on your side."

"Yeah, that's just it. Time's not on my side. I'm not sure what to do."

"Think hard, man. That's all I'm saying," Mike said, looking at Keith intensely.

"Got it," Keith said, and he walked out of Mike's office.

Keith went back to his desk. After staring out the window for a few minutes, he looked at his watch. It was almost 1:30. He picked up the phone and called Mrs. Nelson at the nursing home.

"This is Jennifer Nelson," the voicemail said. "I'm not available right now. Please leave a message, and I'll get back to you as soon as I can."

"Shit," Keith mumbled as he hung up the phone. His heart yearned to go back to Georgia to see his mother just one more time. But his head was more aligned with his family and his boss, and they were telling him that it wasn't practical.

He dialed the nursing home number again.

"Hello. This is Jennifer."

"Hi, Mrs. Nelson. It's Keith Clay."

"Hey, Keith. Good to hear from you again. How is it in California? It's raining cats and dogs here."

"Fine." Keith took a breath. "Mrs. Nelson, how's Mildred doing?"

"Your mother's condition isn't too good. She's on an IV, and we're administering morphine for the pain."

Keith knew what that looked like. Four years prior, he'd watched his mother-in-law die from cancer in her home in Idaho. It was the first time he'd seen a person die.

For nearly a minute, there was silence as he processed the message.

Finally, he said, "I understand. But she could be this way for a few weeks, right?"

"I really can't say."

"A few years ago, my mother-in-law died from cancer. We brought her home for her final days, and she was unconscious for weeks before she passed. So maybe I have some time."

"What are you saying?"

"It isn't possible for me to get back there until the sixteenth. So I'm hoping she'll still be with us then. Do you agree?"

There was an audible exhale on the other end of the phone. "I'm sorry, Keith. I don't want to give you false hope."

"But it's possible, right?"

"Well, yes. It's possible."

"I'll have to take that for now," Keith said. "Listen, say a prayer for her. I'll see you on the sixteenth."

"Okay, we'll all say a prayer for you and your mother. Bye now, Keith."

"Bye, Mrs. Nelson."

After hanging up the phone, Keith looked up and saw Lynn standing in the doorway.

"Haven't seen you all day," she said. "Everything alright?"

"Meetings all morning—budgets and ERP stuff. Then I had lunch with Mike."

Lynn came into his office and sat down across from his desk. "You look stressed. You okay?"

"Yeah, I'm fine."

"Really?"

Keith sighed, "I want to go back. I want to see her again, but I can't right now, and I'm struggling. Why am I even asking the question? Anybody else would be on a plane right now. They wouldn't take a second to debate it." Keith waved his arms. "But here I am, sitting and asking the nursing home to keep her alive until it's convenient for me to get back there. What's wrong with me?"

"Aren't you being a little hard on yourself? Most people who've had the type of history you've had with your mother wouldn't have bothered to go see her at all. You not only went, but you also had a beautiful experience." Lynn flipped a hand around while she listed things out. "You didn't put pressure on her or on yourself to conjure up some kind of emotional miracle and reconcile all the bad blood and rough moments. You should be proud of yourself for that." She smiled. "It wasn't that long ago you were sitting in my office arguing with me about going to see her. But you went, and it was a wonderful thing. You should be at peace with yourself, not beating yourself up."

"Yeah, Mike said I should enjoy the one wonderful moment I had with her."

"He did?" Lynn chuckled. "That's probably the only thing we agree on. But the fact that Mike and I are both telling you the same thing means maybe you should listen."

"Yeah. Maybe."

"Oh, you're so stubborn sometimes."

"Steadfast," Keith corrected. "I'm not stubborn. Just steadfast."

Both laughed.

Keith stood up, extended his hand across the desk, and shook hands with Lynn. "You do make me think. Now, let's talk about Australia's volume," he said as he returned to his seat.

On his way home that night, his cell phone rang. It was Fern.

"Just calling to remind you that it's time for you to come see me," she said. "I want to hear about your visit."

"You bet. I'll come up Saturday, and I'll call you when I'm a half hour out," Keith replied. "How are you feeling?"

"Not bad for an eighty-two-year-old fat lady." She paused. "I don't want to keep you long. I just wanted to see if you were coming up. I do love our visits, you know."

"I know. I do too. See you Saturday," Keith said, and he hung up after she said bye.

***

Saturday morning was a little on the cool side but plenty warm enough to ride the Harley up to Palmdale. After having cereal and a couple of cups of coffee in the kitchen, Keith went upstairs to change.

While coming out of her bedroom, his wife saw him and asked, "You going to Fern's today?"

"Yeah. She called me to remind me Thursday."

"She okay?"

"I think so. We haven't talked since I got back from Georgia, so she wants to hear about the visit."

"Well, tell her hello for me," she said and then turned and went downstairs, the trio of poodles and the Pomeranian right behind her.

Keith was relieved the exchange didn't erupt into a fight. It didn't take much those days.

On his way out the door, he pulled the notepad with questions out of his briefcase and tucked it inside his leather jacket. He replayed the questions and answers in his head during the entire ride to Fern's.

Fern met Keith at the door. Ed waved from his corner. Fern and Keith assumed their usual positions.

"How have you been?" Fern asked.

"Eh, alright. Work has been busy, but that's been easier than dealing with things at home."

"What's going on there?"

Keith shrugged. "Beth and I aren't talking much. When I told her I was going to Georgia, she got pissed and told me I was a fool." He cracked his knuckles and sighed. "Since then, we've barely said a word to each other. We don't even eat together anymore. I come home, grab something from the fridge, pour a big glass of wine, and eat in the garage while watching TV."

"It must be tough. But how do you feel about the visit? Was it worth the grief at home?" Fern asked, fixing her eyes on Keith.

Keith smiled at Fern and said, "Oh yeah. Let me tell you about it."

Keith began sharing the details of his visit with his mother the week before. When he got to the part about him asking his mother the questions, he read them from the notepad and explained her answers. He and Fern both cried when he got to the questions about his father.

"It's sad she didn't recognize you," Fern said as she blew her nose into a tissue and then pulled another one out of her bra.

"In a way, it was better," Keith said. Then he added, "I'm not sure who she thought she was talking to, but she answered easily and, I think, more honestly than she may have if she knew it was me asking the questions. A big part of me thinks she would've given answers she wanted me to have or answers she thought I wanted." He shrugged. "At first, I was a little bugged by it, but then I remembered why I was there in the first place: to get to know her and provide some comfort to a dying woman."

Those last words prompted full-on tears from both.

Fern held out her arms to Keith. He moved beside her on the sofa, put his arms around her and his head on her shoulder, and cried like a baby.

When the tears subsided, Keith went back to his chair. After sitting down, he stared at the notepad. The room was silent except for the faint sounds coming from the TV.

"You're going to have to find a safe place for that," Fern said, breaking the silence.

"For what?"

"The notepad. You have to keep that forever. Be sure to date it and take it out from time to time and recall that moment. The last moment."

"I don't want it to be the last."

"What do you mean?"

"I'm going back to be with her as soon as I get back from China," Keith said. "I've booked a flight from LAX. Won't even go home. Just get off one plane and get on another."

"What's your mother's condition?"

"She's on morphine and an IV. Mrs. Nelson can't tell me how long she's got, of course. But Jackie was in that state for a few weeks before she passed."

Fern just looked at Keith for a long minute.

"What?" he finally asked.

"It's funny to think that a couple of weeks ago, you were here telling me how useless it would be to go see her. Somehow, you got your head around it and went back to experience a wonderful moment." Fern smiled. "You didn't turn out so bad, Keith Clay. I'm proud of you, and I love the way you tell the story. You do talk 'purdy.'"

Fern and Keith continued talking a while longer, but when Fern started to get tired, they called it a day, and Keith left for home. On the way back to Carlsbad, Keith enjoyed the sun hitting his face and the wind bouncing off his body. From the bottom of his toes to the top of his head, he just felt good. Fern always had a way of lifting his spirits.

But as he turned into his neighborhood, a dark thought came to him: *How long before Fern's in the same state as Mother?*

Keith waved his hand in front of his face and turned his thoughts elsewhere. He needed a drink, or at least he was determined to have one and a cigar.

The next morning, Keith got up early to get ready for his trip. After a shower, he got dressed and went downstairs. He placed his bag and briefcase by the front door and headed for the kitchen to get a cup of coffee before the limo arrived to take him to LAX.

As he poured his coffee, the family cat, Mattie, came around as she normally did in the morning, looking to be fed. Keith opened a can of cat food and put half of the contents into her food bowl on top of the counter. Mattie watched him patiently. He looked at the cat and smiled.

She meowed as though to say, "Let's skip the morning friendly exchange and get on with the feeding. I'm hungry. You know the routine, buddy."

"Yes, sweetheart, I know what you want. Here you go," Keith said as he slid the dish over to her.

Just then, he received a text letting him know the car was out front.

Visits to China had been occurring about every six weeks that year, so they'd become pretty routine. In the beginning, it was exciting, and the family would come outside, give goodbye kisses, and wave as he pulled away. Since then, his daughters had gotten busy with their own lives, and even though his relationship with Beth was rocky before, it had only gotten worse in the last few weeks.

As the car pulled away, Keith looked back at the house and, for a brief second, imagined he saw his wife and daughters waving at him in their pajamas. But it was only in his head. He texted his wife, saying that he was on his way to the airport and that he would call once he got settled in the lounge.

Just as he put his phone back in the chest pocket of his sport coat, it rang.

Looking down at it, he saw it was an unknown caller. For some reason, a feeling of dread came over him.

On the fourth ring, he answered. "Keith here."

"Keith, this is Jennifer Nelson. Sorry to bother you so early on a Sunday, but I'm afraid I have some bad news. Your mother passed this morning. Our nurses were with her in her last moments, so she wasn't alone." She paused. "I'm so sorry to have to tell you this. I know you were hoping she could hang in there until you got back, but her time has come. I'm so sorry."

For a second, there was silence. Keith had already been feeling a little down just before the call. His heart sank even deeper.

"Keith? Are you still there?" Mrs. Nelson asked.

"Yes, I'm here." He sighed. "This is a disappointment. I was hoping to be there for her one more time."

"I know, and I think you're wonderful for wanting that. But she's gone now. She's in a better place, and you should feel good for putting a smile on her face."

"Thank you, Mrs. Nelson."

"Please, call me Jennifer."

"Okay, Jennifer." Keith took a deep breath and then got down to business. "Where is she now? What arrangements have been made?"

"The funeral home picked her up just a few minutes ago. Your uncle JB was here and took care of the paperwork and financial obligations."

"Okay, but what are the arrangements?"

"I don't know. Your uncle didn't share that with me. Perhaps you can call him."

"Oh. I'll get with my brother, and he'll find out."

"Is there anything else I can do for you, Keith?"

"No, Jennifer. You've been very helpful. I appreciate the call. Thank you for all you've done."

"You're welcome. It's been a real pleasure. Your mama was proud of you, I'm sure. Bye now."

Keith hung up and then called his brother.

It went to voicemail.

"Fuck. What the hell's he doing that's more important than taking a call from his bother?" Keith asked himself out loud.

He dialed the number again with the same result, and two more attempts met the same end.

"Let go. Calm down," Keith said to himself and put the phone back in his chest pocket.

Traffic was light, and they were making good time. The limo was only thirty minutes from LAX. Keith's phone rang. "Keith here," he answered.

"Hey, Keith. It's Robbie. Sorry I missed your call. What's up?"

"Robbie, Jennifer from the nursing home called me. Mother passed."

"She just called me too. Mama was on morphine and had been on her way out for the past few days, she told me." Robbie took a deep breath. "Well, it's over now. She doesn't have to suffer anymore."

"Yes, no more suffering. Hey," Keith said, remembering about the arrangements, "can you call JB and see what services are planned and where she's going to be buried?"

"Why?"

"'Why,' what? We should know what's going to happen to her."

"Why?"

"Are you serious?" Keith rolled his eyes. "I want to know what's going to happen to her. What were her wishes? Where is she going to be buried? Is she *going* to be buried?" He huffed. "I can't believe you don't want to know."

"I can't believe you *want* to know. For the last few years, you haven't wanted to know anything about where she is or what she's doing." Robbie snorted. "In fact, it's been that way for the last three fucking decades or more. Now, all of a sudden, you want to know."

"Don't you?"

"No. I don't. It ain't any of my business, and it hasn't been for a long time. It took me a while to figure that out, but I did."

"That's shitty, Robbie. Just shitty. You were closer to her than I was. I would've thought you'd care about the final arrangements."

"Fuck you, Keith. You had a good moment with her, and that's great. But she didn't even know who you were. You got to know who her best friend was and that she loved Dad. But she didn't know who she was talking to." Robbie huffed. "Now you act like all the years that have passed didn't happen. All the pain, all the drunken phone calls where she called you every name in the book, and the fact that she didn't give a shit about us unless she was in trouble is just somehow okay now. She didn't say thank you once when we went to New Jersey."

Keith threw a hand up as he spoke. "We should care now. That's all I'm saying. We need to pay our last respects."

"Where are you now? You sound like you're in a car."

"I am. Heading to Hong Kong. Back next Sunday. Can you call JB and find out what the arrangements are? That's all I'm asking."

Robbie sighed. "Keith, you're asking more than you know."

"Well, will you do it for me?"

"No. You call JB. Mom's dead, and that chapter of our life is over once and for all. Calling JB will just open up a can of worms and bring on more shit to deal with than I have time for or got interest in. Sorry if that sounds cold, Keith." Robbie exhaled sharply. "You call if you dare. Good luck with that shit. My suggestion is that you go to China, bury yourself in work during the day, and toast her with whatever the fuck they drink in China. But that's it. Move on, man. Just move on. I am," Robbie said, then hung up.

Keith sat in silence, absorbing the news that she was really gone. He wouldn't be able to see her another time, and it left him wondering, *Who was she?*

"Tom Bradley Terminal, Mr. Clay," the driver said as they pulled in front of the airport.

Chapter 10: A Better Place

Months passed, and Keith never called his uncle. His brother's words rang true: calling his uncle would only pull him into another battle, and he'd already had enough of them to manage. For a while, he felt guilty, but eventually, that faded.

His experience with his mother and his struggle with the aftermath, along with the continued issues at home, became a big part of his almost weekly visits with Fern. Miraculously, she seemed to be getting better. He was thankful for that.

Work was becoming more challenging, and Keith stepped up his game to meet those demands. They culminated in an opportunity he wasn't expecting: the company had bought two businesses in the UK and was in discussions to buy more in Europe. Within a few months, he was asked to move to England, lead the integration of the two UK businesses, and run them for a couple of years. Even though he knew the step might be a one-way ticket, he agreed to take it on.

Beth supported the idea, partly because she knew it was a good move for Keith in the company and partially because it would allow her to be alone for a few months.

"Yeah, I'm moving to England," Keith told his brother over the phone on his way to work one morning.

"Is that good?"

"Yes, it's great. The companies are in Bristol and Hereford, two hours or so west of London. I'll work out of Hereford."

"Is Beth going too?"

"Yes, she'll join me after I get things settled. Jackie will stay at the house, but both the girls will come visit, of course." He paused, thinking, then said, "Hey, I'd like to come see you before I leave the States. I booked a flight for next weekend. I fly in Friday. We can hang out Friday night and Saturday. That work for you?"

"I'll make it work. I look forward to seeing you."

***

The weather in Georgia was cold and rainy. When Keith got to Robbie's house, he was glad to see Robbie was already home. The two hugged and patted each other on the back when he entered the house.

"Come on," Robbie said. "I got us set up in my new man cave. Just leave your bags here." Robbie guided Keith down the hall to the door leading to the garage.

Keith saw that the remodeling Robbie had been doing in the house had continued into the garage. One side was taken up with his truck and tools. The other bay had been converted into a cigar lounge. A high bar table with two stools, a leather sofa, and a coffee table made from an old truck rim with a glass top all sat on a large area rug. A bar sat along the wall with mirrored panels behind shelves that were stocked with a variety of bourbons and vodkas. Several old automotive stickers covered a small refrigerator in the corner. On the walls were posters of scantily clad, buxom women. Tucked in the corner, a large space heater supplied adequate warmth.

"How do you like it?" Robbie asked. "Ain't it cool?"

"Looks great! You've outdone yourself." Keith motioned to the bar. "How about a drink, barkeep?"

They settled at the high table, ate pizza, and drank bourbon. After they'd finished the pizza, they settled on the fake leather sofa and lit cigars.

Since the call on the day their mother passed, they had made up and talked at least once a month, so there wasn't much to catch up on. Keith had brought old photo albums, and they spent the rest of the evening going down memory lane, with the photos serving as corrections or confirmations of each other's memories.

After several cigars and nearly a full bottle of Maker's, the time to end the pleasant evening drew nearer, so Keith and Robbie began to discuss plans for the next day.

"Well," Keith said. "You know that tour we did last time I was here?"

"Yeah. You want to do that shit again?"

"Yep. But we can take a bottle this time instead of beer. I don't know when I'll be back this way."

"Okay. Don't get all sad on me," Robbie said, shrugging. "I'll go. No problem."

The sun rose late in the morning that time of year, and the two men were glad of it. Neither wanted nor felt a need to get up early. After Robbie made a breakfast of scrambled eggs, sausage, and toast, the two headed out.

They followed the same route they'd taken months before. At their grandfather Clay's gravesite, they made two toasts because they couldn't agree on a single. "To the best grandfather and a good friend," was Robbie's toast. "To the biggest asshole but a fun guy?" was Keith's. At their grandmother's gravesite, they both agreed on the same toast: "To a hardworking woman who lived a simple life with simple expectations."

After the toast, Keith said, "You know, it's funny and sad. Her expectations *were* simple. Yet her disappointments were great."

"Yes, she had many. But she kept going, and she didn't blame anyone even though she could have," Robbie said. "Hey, let's toast the rest of the Smith and Clay family buried in this cemetery. There *are* a bunch of them."

The two held their shot glasses up, clanged them together, and took a drink to their ancestors' relatives.

Then, they continued to the last stop of the day: the Lanhams' gravesite, the one for their mother's parents. They pulled up to the little church and said a toast to their grandparents in the car out of respect for the fact that their grandparents wouldn't have approved of the booze—and since it was raining.

After a few minutes, the rain subsided, and Keith and Robbie got out and started walking up the hill toward the sites, with Keith leading the way. The two gravestones came into view.

Keith stopped and looked down. What he saw surprised him. "Robbie, hurry!" he said. "Come see this."

Robbie was a heavy smoker and was out of breath by the time he arrived at Keith's side. "What, what is it?" he asked.

"Look."

Both of them looked down at a small headstone placed between their grandparents. It read, *Daughter. Mildred L. Harvey, Sept 1, 1939– Apr 9, 2012.*

For a long time, the two just stood and stared down at the small marker.

Finally, Keith said, "Let's say a prayer."

Both men said a silent prayer to their mother, grandfather, and grandmother. When they opened their eyes, the two put their arms around each other and continued to take in the moment.

Robbie wiped a tear with his sleeve and said, "Let's go, Keith."

Keith agreed, and they turned to walk down the hill back toward the car. Along the way, the sun popped through an opening in the clouds.

At the bottom of the hill, they stopped at the car and looked up at the sun beaming through the hole the clouds made for it. Keith looked up the hill toward the gravesite, then up at the sun, and he smiled.

"She's in the right place," Keith said. "She's in a better place."

ABOUT THE AUTHOR

Mike Fuqua was born in Landstuhl, Germany, on an American military base. When his father switched careers to aerospace, the family moved to rural Georgia, where Mike developed his passion for airplanes, motorcycles and a good story.

After earning both an undergraduate and graduate degree, he became a supply chain executive serving the hardware and home-improvement market. His career presented several opportunities to live all over the US and Europe.

Mike has two daughters. His wife, Andrea, and their two cats, Gracie and Frankie live in Redlands California. Sharing experiences about facing life's challenges inspires his writing, and he wants readers to know that even though we don't always have everything figured out, our challenges offer us the chance to learn, laugh, and love.

ABOUT THE AUTHOR

Mike Fuqua was born in Landstuhl, Germany, on an American military base. When his father switched careers to aerospace, the family moved to rural Georgia, where Mike developed his passion for airplanes, motorcycles and a good story.

After earning both an undergraduate and graduate degree, he became a supply chain executive serving the hardware and home-improvement market. His career presented several opportunities to live all over the US and Europe.

Mike has two daughters. His wife, Andrea, and their two cats, Gracie and Frankie live in Redlands California. Sharing experiences about facing life's challenges inspires his writing, and he wants readers to know that even though we don't always have everything figured out, our challenges offer us the chance to learn, laugh, and love.

www.ingramcontent.com/pod-product-compliance
Lightning Source LLC
Chambersburg PA
CBHW030150200626
46812CB00016B/1773